"Honey, Wake Up And Feed The Baby," Joe Said.

It struck him that for a single man who intended to stay that way, he was beginning to sound dangerously domestic. Downright paternal, in fact.

And then he heard something that slammed him in the belly like a fist.

Sophie whimpered in her sleep, and Joe groaned. He touched her lightly on the arm, just enough to rouse her.

In the second before she awakened, she was totally vulnerable.

In that moment, Joe knew that he could no more walk out and leave her—leave her and her baby—than he could fly to the moon. It was even worse admitting he could be turned on by a woman who had just given birth to another man's baby. Either he was totally depraved, or the human instinct for survival and reproduction was a hell of a lot stronger than he'd suspected.

Dear Reader,

Happy Holidays to all of you from the staff of Silhouette Desire! Our celebration of Desire's fifteenth anniversary continues, and to kick off this holiday season, we have a wonderful new book from Dixie Browning called *Look What the Stork Brought*. Dixie, who is truly a Desire star, has written over sixty titles for Silhouette.

Next up, *The Surprise Christmas Bride* by Maureen Child. If you like stories chock-full of love and laughter, this is the book for you. And Anne Eames continues her MONTANA MALONES miniseries with *The Best Little Joeville Christmas*.

The month is completed with more Christmas treats: *A Husband in Her Stocking* by Christine Pacheco; *I Married a Prince* by Kathryn Jensen and *Santa Cowboy* by Barbara McMahon.

I hope you all enjoy your holidays, and hope that Silhouette Desire will add to the warmth of the season. So enjoy the very best in romance from Desire!

Melissa Senate

Senior Editor

Please address questions and book requests to:
Silhouette Reader Service
U.S.: 3010 Walden Ave., P.O. Box 1325, Buffalo, NY 14269
Canadian: P.O. Box 609, Fort Erie, Ont. L2A 5X3

DIXIE BROWNING

LOOK WHAT THE STORK BROUGHT

LOOK WHAT THE STORK BROUGHT

Copyright © 1997 by Dixie Browning

SILHOUETTE *Desire®*

Published by Silhouette Books
America's Publisher of Contemporary Romance

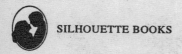

SILHOUETTE BOOKS

ISBN 0-373-76111-2

LOOK WHAT THE STORK BROUGHT

DIXIE BROWNING

celebrated her sixtieth book for Silhouette with the publication of *Stryker's Wife* in 1996. She has also written a number of historical romances with her sister under the name Bronwyn Williams. A charter member of Romance Writers of America and a member of Novelists, Inc., Browning has won numerous awards for her work. She divides her time between Winston-Salem and the Outer Banks of North Carolina.

One

He was closing in. So close he could almost smell blood. Lifting one hand from the steering wheel, Joe Dana pinched the place between his eyes where it throbbed. It was just past ten on a steamy July morning, and he'd pulled over onto the side of the road. Briefly, he'd considered checking into a hotel, catching a shower and a few hours' sleep first, but he was too close. After going flat out for the past five weeks—the last twenty-two hours of it without sleep—he wanted only to wind things up and go home.

Wherever home was. At the moment, it was a storage unit in Fort Worth. That and some unfinished plans.

For the time being, he'd seen enough sheriffs and small-town cops to last him a while. As for women hanging all over him, soaking his shirt with their tears, he could do without those, too.

He yawned again, inhaling the stale aroma of his own sweat and too many fast-food containers. Once this gig was finished, he was going to the best hotel in town to soak his carcass in hot water for a few hours, send his boots out to be polished, his laundry out to be finished, order in a slab of beef, cooked just the way he liked it, with a basket of fries, a gallon of milk and half-a-gallon of ice cream....

And then he was going to sleep for a week.

The slip of paper with instructions to the Bayard woman's house said turn right off Highway 158 onto the first dirt road past Frenchman's Creek; pass a mobile home on the left, a log tobacco barn on the right, go a mile farther and look for a mailbox mounted on a busted hay-rake.

"Can't miss it," the deputy had said. "Last place on the road. County don't gravel past there. She wanted for something? Heard she worked in a bank in town till she moved to Davie County a few months back. I went and got a raccoon out of her attic, first week she moved in. Seemed like a real nice woman, but these days you never know, do you?"

No, thought Joe, you never know. He didn't know if she was the brains of the organization—if there even was an organization, instead of just a one-man scam—or one more in a long line of tearful victims.

He did know that the eighteenth-century jade vase she'd described in *The Antique and Artifact Trader* was a part of the collection he'd been tracking all the way from Dallas. He'd picked up the trail in Amarillo, lost it in Guymon, found it again in Tulsa and chased it all the way to North Carolina. Along the way, he'd checked out every pawn shop, every law enforcement office and heard more sob stories than any broken-down ex-cop needed to hear when he was officially retired.

He had a hunch about this one, though. A strong feeling that he was finally closing in.

Then again, the feeling could be just the result of too many chili dogs. As for his headache, that was a result of too many hours behind the wheel. His knee was killing him—also the result of driving too long without a break.

On the other hand, it was usually at a time like this, when he was scraping the bottom of the barrel, that his luck suddenly took a turn for the better. Hell, he'd been flat on his back in a hospital bed when he'd thought of the one thing they'd overlooked in the Drayton case. Once he was back on his feet again, he'd been able to wrap things up. All three brothers were indicted and behind bars, and he'd earned him-self another commendation to go with his early retire-ment papers.

Joe yawned again, then pulled onto the highway and turned right on the graveled state road. A mile or so farther, he turned off onto a rutted, weed-cluttered driveway. The house looked like a few million other old farmhouses. Four rooms up, four down, with a one-story shoot off the back. This one had flowers. Vine-covered trellises at each end of the porch and blooming beds underneath the windows. Crook or not, the lady had a way with plants.

He pulled up in front, set the parking brake and eased himself out of the cab, moving stiffly until he worked out a few kinks. Before he even reached the front door he had a feeling the house was empty, but he knocked anyway, because it was the polite thing to do.

Knocked twice and waited. And then his instincts kicked in. It was called situation awareness, and his was usually right on target when it came to sensing if a house was really empty or if somebody was in there hiding, ready to blow his head off.

This one was empty. He'd bet his best boots on it. Quietly he eased down off the porch and headed around back. With or without a badge, he wasn't into breaking and entering, but if the back door just happened to be open...

And then he saw her and stopped dead in his tracks, staring over the chicken-wire fence. His first thought was that she was big. His second, that she was a genuine blond. No dark roots. His third, that she was in trouble, which was an indication of just how tired he was. Normally in a situation like this, he'd have taken her vitals by now, and might even be administering mouth-to-mouth.

She was lying flat on the ground—or as flat as possible under the circumstances—in some kind of a garden. Rows of growing stuff, mostly vegetables. Her knees were bent, there was a big floppy hat with a sunflower on the brim resting on one of them, and a pile of weeds beside her left elbow. Her face looked flushed to him, like she was either feverish or she'd been out in the sun too long.

Heatstroke? Possibly. The temperature was hovering around the century mark, with the humidity not far behind.

Her eyes were closed. Both her hands were resting on top of a belly so big it hiked her skirt halfway up her thighs.

As for the thighs, they were long, firm and tanned. Just for the record.

Long years of training kicked in before he could actually start drooling. Moving swiftly to her side, he let himself inside the fence, mentally skimming files of all the things that could go wrong with a woman who looked to be about twelve months pregnant. He was halfway down on his good knee, reaching for her pulse when she opened her eyes and smiled up at him.

It was the smile that froze him in a muscle-killing crouch. It was slow, sleepy and nowhere near as wary as it should have been, under the circumstances. "Do I know you?" she murmured.

"Are you all right?" He settled on his knees, ignoring the stiffness and the hard, rocky ground. The Ch'ien Lung vase had waited this long—it could wait a few minutes more.

"I'm not real sure." Her voice was like her smile, sort of slow and sleepy. And sweet.

"You're, ah...lying down?" *In other words, why the devil are you lying down in the middle of the yard, in the middle of the morning?*

"My back hurt. I was weeding, but it's so hot. Who are you? If you're selling something, I'm afraid I can't buy. If you've come about my car, the garage already called. I'll pick it up Monday, if that's all right."

"I'm not selling, and I don't know anything about your car. If you're Ms. Sophie Bayard, I'd like to—"

"Help me up, will you? I'm clumsy as an ox these days but if you can get me on my feet, I'll go inside and pour us some iced tea. Lawsy, it's hot, isn't it? What did you say your name was?"

"I didn't, but it's Joe Dana. Ma'am, I'd like to—"

She grabbed the sunflower hat with one hand and held the other one up for him to take. Both hands were dirty. And ringless. Which didn't necessarily mean anything. "Don't hurt yourself, I weigh a ton," she warned.

She was a big girl, all right. Big boned. He figured her for about five foot eight, a hundred-fifty, maybe one fifty-five, at the moment. She was carrying a lot of excess cargo. That denim tent she was wearing looked about ready to give up the ghost.

Joe glanced at the prominent breasts resting on her even more prominent belly and quickly looked away. Funny thing, he'd never before noticed just how *female* a pregnant woman looked.

He got her up off the ground with only a few minor twinges in his bad knee. Her skin had a nice smell. She was hot, dusty, and she'd been working in onions, but underneath all that she had a nice, soapy, womanly, herbal smell. Joe was a noticing man. Too many times his life had depended on just such subtle details.

For one brief moment she leaned against him, and he let himself be leaned on, but then he steadied her and stepped back. It didn't pay to get too friendly with the enemy. It only got in the way of what he had to do, which no longer seemed as simple as it had back when he'd first picked up the lead.

"All right now? Not dizzy or anything, are you?"

"No, I'm just fine except for my back. It—'' She reached back and rubbed down low, and then a startled look came over her face. Joe was watching her closely for any sign of—well, for any sign of anything. Guilt. Shame. Fear. She sure as hell wasn't going to try to run from him, not in her condition.

His eyes narrowed. "What is it?"

"Warm. Wet. Oh, my mercy, something's happened.'' Her eyes got as round as marbles, and Joe noticed their color for the first time. They were gray with a hint of green. Like Spanish moss after a rain.

"You got a cramp? Where? Your leg? Your back?" *Not your belly. Please, lady, not your belly. Don't go into labor on me now...this I don't need!*

"I've wet my pants, and oh—! It's still happening!"

He uttered a profanity under his breath. "Your water just broke. When are you due?"

"My water?"

"Yeah, your water. Don't you know anything?"

"If you mean about having babies, I've never actually had one before, but I went to a few classes at the Y. And I've read all this stuff—you know, about what to expect and all, but—oh, lawsy, this is so embarrassing!''

"Tell me about it," Joe muttered, and calmly went into action. "First thing we're going to do is we're going to get you inside."

She moaned. He didn't think she was actually hurting, just scared, but then, he'd never had a baby. How would he know?

"You can walk, can't you? I can carry you if you think you'll have trouble with the steps, but walking's supposed to be good for a woman at a time like this."

He hoped it was. If he had to carry her, they might both come to grief right here between the onions and the butter beans. Joe was a big man—six-two, a hundred eighty-seven. But he'd been horse-busted, gunshot and otherwise mistreated a few too many times in his thirty-eight-and-a-half years. No sense in pushing his luck.

With his arm to steady her, she made it just fine. She had nice, delicate features, but that jaw of hers told a different story. He might not be able to wind things up here quite as easily as he'd hoped.

"I want to take a real quick shower before I go to the hospital. Will you stand outside the bathroom door so I can call you if I need you?"

Joe was busy looking around, just in case she was dumb enough to keep the stuff right out in plain sight. His grandmother always had, but then, she'd had the right to show it off.

"Are you sure you ought to do this?" he asked. First time or not, she might be one of those women who popped out babies like spitting out watermelon seeds.

"Nothing hurts. I feel fine. In fact, I feel better than I've felt in ages."

"Euphoria."

"I beg your pardon?" But before he could explain that sometimes, even in the midst of a crisis, a feeling of well-being could overcome a body and make him think everything was all right when it wasn't, she was already headed down the hall.

"Can you do it in three minutes?" he asked, going after her.

"Not if I shampoo my hair. Give me five."

"Lady, they're not mine to give. If you get into trouble in there, I'm the one who's going to have to bail you out, and I've got a bad knee, so don't push your luck, all right?"

She beamed at him. Positively beamed. Joe forgot all about her big, gravid belly and her dirty, green-stained, onion-scented hands. And the fact that she was trying to sell off a trinket belonging to his grand-mother that was valued at eighteen grand.

Euphoria. By the time he snapped out of his version, she was barricaded behind the bathroom door. He could hear her humming something that sounded sus-piciously like a lullaby.

"Hand me that bottle of lotion from my dresser, will you? Second door to the left," she called over the sound of rushing water.

Well…not exactly rushing. Trickling would be more like it. He'd already noticed that up close, the house lost some of its bucolic charm and was just an old house, with worn floorboards, rattling window-panes and a couple of wheezing window units fighting a losing battle to overcome the heat and humidity.

He fetched her lotion, and while he was at it, he glanced around the bedroom. Just in case. Joe, after all, was a man with a mission.

Seven hours later he was on his fifth cup of black coffee, which was the last thing he needed, when a nurse wearing scrubs came through to the waiting room. He stood, thinking it was about time, and she came on over.

"Are you Joe?"

"Has she had anything yet?"

"Not yet. She's asking for you again."

As frustrating as it was, Joe had figured it was only common decency to let her have her kid and catch her breath before he got down to business. Not that he'd had much option. Back at the house she'd been too distracted. While she'd timed her pains, he'd asked if she'd ever heard of a Ch'ien Lung vase, and she'd said, oh, that reminded her—she needed to feed her fish.

She had a goldfish. Women were wacky, and broody women were worse than that. He'd given up on getting any reasonable answers and asked if there was anybody he could call for her.

She'd said, yes, he could call her a cab because she might as well go in and stay instead of waiting until the last minute. So he'd made up his mind to stick it out. It wasn't like she could run out on him, not in her condition.

He'd stuck by her, and when the pains were eight minutes apart, he'd helped her climb into his truck, gone back and gotten her suitcase and driven her to the county hospital.

After she was settled in her room and a string of folks wearing white or green had pulled the curtains shut and done whatever it was they had to do, he'd dragged a chair up beside her bed and helped her wait.

He could've questioned her then, but he hadn't. They'd talked about nothing in particular. Her goldfish. He was called Darryl. The weather. It was hot. Her garden—it needed rain. And then the pains started piling in on her, and he'd let her crush his fingers and wished there was more he could do.

Not that it was any of his business, but she needed someone, and nobody else had showed up.

"It won't be long now," he'd told her, hoping to hell he was right. He didn't know how much more of this he could take.

"I think I...left the...back door unlocked," she'd said through clenched teeth.

"I checked. It's locked." She had nice teeth. Not perfect, just nice and white and square. Joe tried to convince himself that she couldn't possibly be involved. In the hospital gown, in spite of a few fine lines at the outer corners of her eyes and a few more across her forehead, she looked more like an overgrown kid than a woman in the process of having a baby.

But she had the goods. She was fencing the stuff. None of the other women he'd talked to had been left with anything. The jerk had seduced them, promised them marriage, cleaned them out and left them, every last one Joe had interviewed, flat broke and either mad as hell or brokenhearted. Or both.

This one was still in possession of the J. J. Dana jade collection. A collection that had been valued at a million and a half nine years ago when the old man had passed away and was probably worth a lot more now. And if she was carrying either a grudge or a torch for the jerk, she covered pretty well.

Once they'd rolled her into the delivery room, Joe had returned to the waiting area. He'd considered going out and finding himself a hotel, figuring he could come back in a day or so, talk to her once she'd had time to settle down and wind things up. There was time. She wasn't going anywhere.

But he hadn't. Instead he'd hung around some more. Waiting.

"Are you the father?" Roughly an hour and forty-five minutes had passed. The woman in scrubs was back.

Not about to get himself thrown out on a technicality, Joe cleared his throat and said, "He couldn't be here. I'm standing in for him. Is she okay? Has she had it yet?"

The nurse shoved a lank chunk of hair back up under her paper hat. "It's a girl. Mother and daughter doing fine. She's been moved to Room 211 and is resting now, but you can see the baby if you want to."

Joe didn't know what to say. It seemed pretty callous to tell her he had no interest in babies, but the truth was, he didn't. He'd delivered a few. Cops occasionally did. Sometimes he'd followed up with a visit, sometimes a donation, but it wasn't his nature to get involved with the people he came into contact with through his work. Not that this case was work, exactly. It was more in the nature of a family obligation. Still...

"Sure," he heard himself saying. "Might as well."

Well, hell—*somebody* had to welcome the little tyke into the world. Once he'd done his duty he would check into that hotel and get something to eat. He'd had enough of machine food to last him a while. Candy bars. Peanuts. Barbecued pork rinds. One of these days he was going to have to get started on a health food and exercise regimen. Maybe after he wound up this business for his grandmother, Miss Emma, and returned home.

TWO

She was no beauty, he'd say that for her. Practically bald, with a red face, fat cheeks and a sour expression, she looked like a bird that had fallen out of the nest about a week too soon. You had to feel sorry for something like that.

"Hi there, Fatcheeks," Joe whispered, after checking around to be sure no one was close enough to see him making a fool of himself. There was an elderly couple ogling the runt on the end and a man with his necktie dangling from his shirt pocket making goo-goo noises at the bundle in the crib three rows down. Assured that no one was paying him any mind, he relaxed. "You gave your mama a pretty rough time, you know that?"

It occurred to him that looking after a newborn infant wasn't going to be any cinch for the Bayard woman. Did she have any friends? Any family? What would she have done if he hadn't happened along when he had?

She'd have gotten along just fine, he told himself quickly, because he needed to believe it. She didn't strike him as the helpless type. She wasn't neurotic. She wasn't sleeping under a bridge out on I-40. He'd learned a lot about her while she talked her way through labor. She'd grown up in an orphanage. Still—if things got tough, there were agencies she could call on. She was bound to have somebody. Nobody was completely alone.

So he'd wait until she caught her breath, and then he'd ask her how the devil she'd come to be in possession of a valuable jade collection that belonged to a woman in Texas, and why she was selling it off, piece by piece. And while he was at it, he'd find out what her connection was to the joker who'd cut a swath across the south, leading women into one indiscretion after another, cleaning them out and skipping town.

And he'd get his answers, too. Not for nothing had he been called the Inquisitor, with a capital *I,* back at DPD.

He waggled his fingers against the nursery glass and whispered, "Yeah, life's a pretty tough gig, kiddo, but with a little luck you'll come through it just fine." It didn't particularly bother him that he sounded like a nutcase. The baby couldn't hear him through the glass. Couldn't even see him. Her eyes were swollen shut.

"What you want to do is find yourself a nice farmer and settle down out here in the country where it's pretty and peaceful, make a few babies, have yourself a few laughs—stay out of any major trouble and chances are pretty good you'll make it through okay. Most folks do. It might not seem that way sometimes, but it's the truth."

The infant labeled only Bayard Girl puckered up and began to wave her fists and kick her tightly bundled feet. She opened her mouth, as if she was expecting a worm to be dropped in it, and, feeling helpless, Joe left.

He needed a real meal, a bath and a three-day nap. Then he was going to get to the root of this business before the Bayard woman figured out what he was after and dug in behind her defenses.

It was a wonder she couldn't tell just by looking at him that he was a cop. Most folks could. His youngest sister, Donna, said it was attitude. Said it stood out all over him, even after he left the force.

But then, both his sisters had proved beyond the shadow of a doubt that they were lousy judges of men.

"Ms. Bayard—when can I see her?" he asked a nurse at the station.

"Are you family?"

He nodded. He was his sisters' brother and Miss Emma's only grandson. "I was just down the hall looking at the baby. She's really something, isn't she?" Which wasn't an outright lie, either.

"Then you might as well go on in if the door's

open. Supper trays'll be coming around any minute now. After that, they'll bring the babies around.''

On the way to Room 211, Joe lined up his questions in firing order. If she was feeling up to it, he figured there was no real point in postponing the inevitable. The first round would have to go right to the heart of the matter, though, because once she tumbled to the reason he was here asking questions, she'd clam up, guilty or not. One thing he'd seen happen over and over again—a woman who'd just been made a fool of didn't like to talk about it. Protecting her pride, she could come across as guilty as sin. On the other hand, a woman who really was guilty as sin could act as innocent as a preacher's maiden aunt.

In other words, there was no understanding a woman.

"You awake?" He whispered. Her eyes were closed, but Joe had a feeling she wasn't really asleep. He told himself she should have looked like hell, considering she'd just delivered a baby that weighed in at nine pounds, seven ounces. She did look tired, but mostly she just looked vulnerable and innocent and guileless.

He studied her features, telling himself it wasn't really an invasion of privacy because he'd announced his presence. At her best, Sophie Bayard was probably one damned good-looking woman. She wasn't at her best, but there was still something about her worth noticing.

Personally Joe had always preferred peppery little brunettes. Had married one, in fact. But that didn't mean he couldn't appreciate a big, easygoing, sweet-smiling blonde when he happened across one in the line of duty.

Sophie knew he was there. For some reason, she didn't want to face him yet. She felt...raw. But she opened her eyes and even managed a smile. She couldn't remember ever being this tired in her entire thirty-four years. Or hurting the way she'd just hurt. They said she'd forget the pain in a matter of days, that new mothers always did, but she hadn't forgotten it yet.

Besides, she was embarrassed. She'd panicked, which wasn't like her. Normally she was calm and levelheaded to a fault. Everybody said so.

How on earth could she have allowed a perfect stranger to mop her off, change her clothes, drive her to the hospital and sit with her all through her labor? She'd practically broken his fingers, hanging on to him while she waited to be wheeled into the delivery room.

So much for her independent, self-sufficient new life-style.

"I thought you'd be gone by now," she said, her voice huskier than usual. She had a dim recollection of yelling a lot when the pain wouldn't go away. She didn't recall it helping much.

"Nope. Still here. How're you feeling?"

"I hurt," she said, which wasn't what she'd intended to say at all.

"You want me to call somebody?"

"No, just pour me some water, will you?"

He did, and then held her head up off the pillow so she could sip from the straw. "Where does it hurt?"

"Everywhere, mostly. My toenails. My hair really hurts. My…well…like I said, mostly everywhere, but it's getting better."

She remembered making an attempt to braid her hair at some time during the procedure, but then the pains had started piling in hard and heavy and she'd let it go.

"Thank you for staying. You really didn't have to. We'll be just fine now. But thank you." That sounded like a bread-and-butter note written by a second-grader. Her brain was functioning, only she couldn't seem to hook it to her tongue.

"You feel like talking?"

She didn't, but said she did because he'd been so nice and he seemed to want to tell her something. And she owed him, because if he hadn't happened along at the right time she might have had her baby right there in the garden between the onions and the butter beans.

No, of course she wouldn't have. There'd been plenty of time. She would have called a taxi. She would have gotten over her momentary panic and handled everything just fine.

"Have you seen her yet? Isn't she beautiful? I still haven't settled on a name." As tired as she was, she felt all warm and glowy, just thinking about her precious little daughter.

"Yeah, she's really something. Listen—" He looked so fierce. She'd noticed that about him right off, even when she'd been all wrapped up in her own situation. He had a hard face, not a handsome one. Not like Rafe. "Are you up to answering a few questions?" he asked her, and she nodded, wondering how many times his nose had been broken.

"Sure. My mouth's about the only part of me that doesn't hurt. Isn't it funny how something as simple as having a baby can make you feel like you've been in a car wreck? Especially my feet."

Joe reached down and jerked the crisp white spread loose from the mattress. "Your toes are bent. Hospital corners. Always hated 'em, myself."

"Oh, that feels better." She wriggled her toes and smiled at him. "Go ahead, ask away. I'll tell you anything I can, but if it's about—"

The clatter that had started down at the far end of the hall grew louder and stopped right outside her door. Someone brought in a tray, plopped it on the stand at the foot of the bed and left without a word.

"Sink or swim, huh?" Joe said as he rolled the stand into position and then cranked the bed up a few turns.

"They don't have much help. I've been considering maybe applying for a job here myself, once the baby's a little older."

"You a nurse?"

"No, but I can do office work. I can use a computer. I could even help in the kitchen."

"You're out of work?"

"No, not quite. But I'm ready for a change, and they have a nursery here. That's a big plus."

"Mmm-hmm." Joe lifted the cover off the plate.

He knew hospital food. Texas or North Carolina, it didn't make much difference. Meat loaf was meat loaf. Vanilla pudding was vanilla pudding. "You want me to cut anything up for you?"

"There's nothing wrong with my hands. But thanks. I don't usually act this way, you know. Helpless, I mean. I've been looking after myself ever since I left school, and I've hardly been sick a day in my life. Maybe that's why all this threw me." She took a bite of meat loaf, grimaced and looked for the salt. "What was it you wanted to talk about?"

She threw him off stride. She was supposed to be evasive. Instead she was asking for it, which screwed up his theory.

So he dragged up a chair, sat down and lined up his questions, but before he could begin, she asked one of her own.

"Why did you stay? You don't know me—you certainly weren't under any obligation. Are you from the home? Should I know you? It's been so long... I've kept up with a few classmates, but they're all girls. Well, women, now."

She sipped her coffee, and Joe made a few mental notes and got set to try again.

And again, she beat him to it. "Want my corn bread? It's dry, but there's some... well, I don't suppose it's butter, but it's something, anyway. I could ring for a nurse and see if she could bring you something to drink."

So they talked about the food and whether or not caffeine was any worse than decaf. Joe still hadn't managed to get around to asking her if she was the brains behind Rafe Davis's long string of robberies, or if she'd only acted as his fence when a woman in a lab coat came in and asked him to step outside.

He did, feeling frustrated, but as soon as he went back inside and started to question her again, someone else came along with a clipboard, and he gave up.

Forty minutes later, he had checked into a hotel, ordered room service, set the air-conditioning on max and run himself a tubful of hot water. He'd waited this long. He could wait a few more hours.

The next morning Joe slept through the alarm. Slept until a crack of sunshine sliced through the drawn draperies and drilled through his eyelids.

He ordered pizza for breakfast, did a few of the exercises the physical therapist had promised would put him back in peak working condition and then eased the resulting kinks out of his carcass under a hot needle-spray shower.

He thought about riding out to the house while it was still empty, going over it with a fine-tooth comb and then facing her with the evidence. They could cut through a whole lot of crap that way.

But he didn't. Instead he called his grandmother and asked how she was feeling, and what she'd been up to. Frowning, he listened to her lethargic responses. "Well, look—I'll be headed back in a few days. Right now I'm going to go by the hospital and check on Sophie and the baby. Remember, I told you about her last night? You wouldn't believe how homely she is.

The baby—not Sophie. I thought all babies were supposed to look like the kid in the toilet paper ads.''

Sophie didn't feel like getting out of bed, but then, it wasn't the first time she'd had to do something she didn't want to do. At least this time she had a good reason to get up. They were going home. She was taking Iris Rebecca Bayard home, and then they'd see how much of her old training from the Children's Home she remembered. She used to be pretty good with the babies but that had been a long time ago. Nearly eighteen years.

She could have used another day to rest up and prepare herself for the responsibility of motherhood, but her insurance wouldn't cover it. And thanks to a handsome, smooth-talking rascal who had stolen her heart, her savings, her self-respect and just about everything else of value she possessed, she couldn't swing it on her own.

At least he'd left her with something, although that was purely accidental. If she hadn't taken it to the bank with her that day to show it to her friends and see if it would fit into a deposit box, he would've taken that, too.

She was wearing her old maternity tent. The going-home outfit she'd packed wouldn't fit over her flab and her outrageous bosom. She'd felt like crying, but then they'd brought in her baby and she'd felt wonderful all over again. Tired, aching, but still wonderful. Euphoria, her new friend would've called it.

She had just asked the orderly to call her a cab when

he poked his head around the door and then followed it with a pair of shoulders wide enough to scrape highways. Joe Dana, she decided, was a man who didn't like to reveal too much of himself. Yesterday she'd seen his scars. Before that she'd noticed only that he was big, even bigger than she was. And dark. Black hair shot with gray. Dark eyes that reminded her of the tinted glass some people had in their cars. From the inside you could see out, but those on the outside didn't stand a chance of seeing in.

Even as distracted as she'd been then, and as tired as he'd obviously been, she'd felt his intensity. It was almost audible. Like humming power lines.

"Good morning," she greeted, a self-conscious smile trembling at the corners of her lips. "We never got around to finishing our conversation, did we?"

"You're fixing to go somewhere?"

"Home. I'm already cleared for takeoff, as they say in all the airplane movies. I've never flown. One of these days I'm going to, though."

She beamed at him. He looked baffled, as if he didn't know what she was talking about, which was understandable. She always talked too much when she was nervous. "I just sent someone to call me a cab. The hospital's lending me a car seat for the baby until I can get one of my own. Isn't that nice of them?"

"No need to call a cab, my truck's right outside."

"Oh, but I can't—"

"Sure you can. I've got a vested interest in little Miss Fatcheeks, remember? The least I can do is see her home."

"Well, if you're sure you don't mind. And then you can ask me whatever it was you wanted to ask me."

"Yeah, sure," he said, and saying something about pulling his truck up to the front entrance, he left.

For one crazy moment Sophie started to call him back. Didn't want him to leave her. She told herself it was only postpartum silliness, and that it would pass. She was already forgetting the birth pangs, just as the nurse said she would. In a few days she'd be back at her computer, juggling nursing, diaper changing and writing ad copy for the agency that currently helped pay the bills while she mailed out résumés and tried not to get her hopes too high.

All the same, she wondered just who he was, and why he was still hanging around.

Miss Fatcheeks, indeed! Her name was Iris Rebecca Bayard.

Three

"It was the yard that convinced me. That big old oak tree will be just perfect for a swing. And you saw my garden. In a year or so I'm fixing to fence in the other side to make a play yard. I might even get a few laying hens. Out here in the country, you can keep chickens, you know. It'll be a wonderful place for Iris to grow up." Sophie only hoped she sounded as confident as her words implied as they turned off the highway.

Joe had hardly spoken a word since they'd left the hospital, but then she'd already discovered that he wasn't much of a talker. She'd chattered all the way home because it was what she did when she was nervous, but she was beginning to run out of things to talk about. The truth was, she was feeling less confident with every mile. What on earth had she been thinking of, moving way out here in the country? The closest neighbor was nearly a mile away, and not even particularly friendly. She'd made the mistake of paying a call soon after she'd moved in, and it had been plain from the first that she'd interrupted the grumpy old man in the middle of his morning nap, or something equally important. The first words out of his mouth were that if she was selling something, he wasn't buying. If she was collecting, he wasn't giving anything, either, because he was living on social security and there was dagnabbed little of it.

If her house were to catch on fire, she'd thought at the time, and he happened to see the smoke, he might stir himself to call the fire department. But what if she just needed someone to talk to? What if she needed advice? Looking after a house and a brand-new baby took a certain amount of experience, and she was beginning to think she might've bitten off more than she could chew. Not that she'd had much choice. Once the first domino had fallen, the rest had come tumbling down before she even realized what was happening.

When it came to soaking up guilt, however, Sophie had plenty of experience, dating back to a time when she'd been too young to understand what it meant and had overheard someone say that it was because of her that her father had run off. Since then, she'd collected guilt the way a magnet collects steel filings.

Flies in the house? Her fault. She must've left the window open.

The cake fell? Oops, she must've slammed a door.

Rained all over the Sunday school picnic?

Well. She wasn't quite *that* powerful. All the same, if she'd prayed a little harder, it might not have rained.

Now Joe was frowning, and that was probably her fault, too. She'd allowed him to drive her home when she could easily have called a cab. It would have cost a fortune, but any day now she'd be hearing from the ad she'd put in the paper. Last time, she'd taken the whole set to an antique dealer to have it appraised, and he'd offered her five thousand dollars for the lot. Thank goodness she'd had sense enough not to be taken in. He'd ended up paying her twice that for one eensy-weensy piece that looked like something you could buy at Walmart. She'd been patting herself on the back ever since.

She'd also learned a lesson. The stuff might be tacky, but it was valuable. And it was hers. Rafe had given it to her, and dead or not, he owed her something for all the things he'd stolen. Not to mention child support.

She slanted a glance at the man beside her. He looked as if he had something on his mind.

Well, of course he did. He'd told her that yesterday, when he'd strolled into her garden and gotten trapped into playing Good Samaritan. He might be frowning now—he might try to act tough, but she knew better. Underneath it all he was a kind, decent man. The kind of man a woman trusted instinctively. The kind with a good heart.

And she was even getting used to his face. It was interesting, with all the sharp edges and angles. It was certainly masculine. And strong. And at the moment, scowling.

"You wanted to ask me something?" Heaven help her if it was about her taxes. She'd always done them herself and never had a smidge of trouble, but along about April 15 of this year she'd been in no frame of mind to concentrate on filling out forms.

At least not government forms. Her own had filled out so fast it had boggled the mind.

"It'll keep," he muttered.

"Are you headed back to Texas?"

"What makes you think I'd be going to Texas?"

"You have Texas plates. And you mentioned staying at a hotel, so I didn't think you were from around here."

"Right."

Right, which? That he was from Texas, or that he'd be going back? She didn't want him to go. And if that wasn't scary, she didn't know what was. Any woman who'd been stupid enough to believe that a handsome, charming scamp like Rafe Davis could take one look at her and fall head over heels in love, needed her head examined. He'd told her she was his golden goddess, and she'd wanted so desperately to believe him she'd let herself be taken in.

Stupid. That said it all. Here she'd been on her own since she was sixteen-and-a-half, and she hadn't learned anything at all about men. There was probably a psychological term for women who allowed themselves to be hornswoggled, but she didn't want to hear it, she really didn't. At the rate she was going, she'd probably be first in line to buy that oceanfront lot in Arizona if the right man offered it for sale.

Instead the wrong man had come along and offered something entirely different, and she'd bought it. And before she'd come to her senses, the skunk had ransacked her jewelry box, turned her closet inside out, stolen her bank card and her three-year-old car, driven to the nearest ATM and cleaned out her account.

And kept on going. Three weeks later he had driven her car into the side of a passenger train down in Georgia.

But he'd left her with something far more valuable than anything he'd taken. Iris. Her baby. Her *family.*

Not to mention all those tacky little jade whatnots that were worth a fortune.

Joe cleared his throat. From the baby seat between them, Iris smacked her gums without waking up. "Joe, what was it you wanted to ask me?" *Let the man state his business and leave, Sophie. You don't need a crutch to lean on, you only think you do.*

"Have you got a crib? Some kind of baby bed?"

"Better than that, I have a complete nursery all painted, furnished and ready to receive. Almost the first thing I did when I leased the house was fix a place for her. I knew my ladder-climbing, paint-smelling days were numbered."

Sophie laughed. Joe didn't. So far he'd proved to be kind, helpful and dependable, but a barrel of laughs he was not.

She thought he might be a policeman, from a few things he'd said while he'd been seeing her through her labor. Now, why on earth would a Texas police-man want to ask her anything? She'd never even been west of the Blue Ridge Mountains.

Unless it had something to do with Rafe. As far as she knew, Rafe had never been to Texas, either. But then, what did she know about the man? He'd told her he was in the commodities business and like a dunce, she hadn't even asked him what kind of commodities he dealt in. By the time he left and she'd had to report the robbery to the sheriff, she wished she'd been a little more wary. And six weeks after that, when the two men had come out to tell her that her car had been found totaled and that the thief was dead, she'd been too dazed from losing her job and learning that she was pregnant. Most of what they'd said had gone in one ear and out the other.

Joe pulled up beside the house and cut the engine. "Looks like rain."

"There's not a cloud in the sky. Listen, I'll pay you back for the diapers and all the rest," Sophie said earnestly. "I'd planned to do my last-minute shopping next week. I get paid on Monday."

"No problem. Call it a baby present."

"You're more of a present than a boxcar full of diapers. Honestly, Joe, I'll never be able to thank you for all you've done. If you hadn't come along—"

"You'd have picked up the phone and called some-one else and everything would have turned out just fine."

"I know that," she said with a certainty she didn't feel.

Call who? The few friends who hadn't moved away were in Winston, at work. She couldn't have asked any of them to walk out in the middle of a workday, drive all the way out to Davie County, hold her hand while she timed her pains, drive her to the hospital and stay with her until she delivered, and then come back the next day and drive her home again. "All the same, it was a nice thing to do. I guess policemen have to be jacks-of-a-lot-of-different-trades."

"What makes you think I'm a policeman?"

"Aren't you?"

"Not anymore." He'd told her yesterday when she'd questioned him, that he was retired. Before she could ask from what, she'd had another hard pain. "Better let me take the baby, then I'll come back and get the rest of the stuff in. Have you ever thought about getting some decent locks installed? A kid with a paper clip could break into your house in ten seconds flat."

Sophie eased herself gingerly out of the high cab and reached back inside for her purse. "And do what? Rob me blind? In case you hadn't noticed, I don't have anything worth stealing."

"Everybody's got a few valuables. Important papers. Jewelry. Antiques." Carefully he lifted the baby from the car seat and settled her in the crook of his arm.

Sophie labeled the thought that popped into her mind inappropriate and told herself to grow up. "Oh, sure," she said airily. "When it comes to antiques, there's the house itself, only it's not mine yet. Unless the heirs of the woman who owned it stop squabbling, it might never be mine, but I do have a cookbook that belonged to my great-grandmother if that counts as an antique. As for jewelry, my watch came from the drugstore. Everything else went south a long time ago, but I still have a TV that'll pick up four-and-a-half stations when weather conditions are just right.''

Joe didn't even crack a smile. Hardly surprising. Sophie's heart felt like a lump of wet dough. This was it, then. He'd leave in a few minutes. He was certainly under no obligation to stay and help her get settled and cheer her up when she got the blues.

That was probably what ailed her now. Postpartum blues. She'd heard all about it. It was miserable, but hardly terminal.

Forcing herself to smile, she said, ''There's some sliced beef and a Vidalia onion in the refrigerator if you want a sandwich before you go. Here, I'll take her now.'' She held out her arms for the small, pink-wrapped bundle.

Joe handed her over. ''Feeling possessive, are we?''

What she was feeling was happy, tearful and hungry all at the same time. At this rate it might take her emotions even longer to recover from childbirth than it did her body.

''Sure she's not too heavy for you to be carrying? You just got out of the hospital.''

''I carried her for almost nine months.''

''I'd have thought more like twelve.''

''She's a big baby. Twenty-three inches long. I was

twenty-two and weighed over ten pounds when I was born.''

"Your family runs to big babies?"

She shrugged. ''I was an only child. When you're little it's hard to judge sizes. The whole world's ten-feet tall.''

They were standing in the front room. Sophie had painted the walls and hung the curtains from her apartment when she'd moved in. Seeing it now through the eyes of a stranger, it struck her that the new furnishings she'd been so proud of when she'd lived in town weren't quite right for a house in the country. Less glass and wrought iron, more wood and chintz would've been better. She'd sold off one of the jade pieces to lease the house, buy the appliances she'd needed and pay a mover. There'd been little left over for redecorating. Insurance had bought a replacement for her car, but she'd had to settle for a secondhand one. It had given her nothing but trouble ever since. By the time she sold off the next piece, she'd have another stack of bills waiting to be paid, but she was determined to save as much as possible for Iris's future. Wood and chintz would simply have to wait.

Joe continued to watch her, his interest disguised by the lazy-lidded look he'd cultivated over the years. He couldn't quite figure her out, and that bothered him. As a rule he was good at reading people. Give him half an hour, one-on-one, and he could tell you what motivated a particular suspect, whether or not he was hiding anything, how close to breaking he was and just where to apply the pressure to make him bust wide open and spill his guts.

Ms. Bayard appeared to be an open book. Unfortunately it was written in a foreign language. She was tired and edgy, which was only natural. She wasn't a whiner. She'd struck him right off as the kind of woman who looked on the bright side of things, even when the going got rough. In that respect, she reminded him of Miss Emma. Or rather, of the way Miss Emma used to be.

"You got any family?" he asked.

"No."

"Friends?"

"Well, of course I have friends. Everyone has friends."

So where were they? Why hadn't they showed up at the hospital with flowers and pink balloons?

At least she had neighbors. Correction—she had a neighbor. An old boozer who'd turn in his own mother for jaywalking if there was a reward.

He still wasn't sure who the baby's father was. Had a pretty good idea, but he wasn't certain. If it was Davis, as he suspected, then what had their relationship been? Did she know he was dead? Did she know he'd had a wife in Rowlett, a suburb about twenty miles east of Dallas?

"Well, anyway, if you don't want a sandwich, maybe you'd like a cup of coffee. One for the road? It won't take a minute to make a pot, or I have iced tea already made. I don't reckon it's gone cloudy since yesterday." She paused, and a wondering look came over her face. "Just yesterday. When I made that tea, I didn't have any family at all, and now look at me—I'm a mother!"

Joe tucked his questions back into a mental file and managed to scrape up what passed for a smile these days. It was easier than he'd expected. She looked so damned earnest with her tired eyes, her frowsy hair and her baggy dress. "You're mighty eager to get rid of me."

"You're welcome to stay as long as you want, of course, but I know you're anxious to get on with— well, whatever. Anyway, I'm truly beholden to you. I don't know what I would've done if—"

He cut her off. Dammit, now she was making him feel guilty.

Holding the baby in one arm, she went and shook a few flakes into the aquarium. "Hi there, Darryl. Look what I brought home," she said softly.

"I could've done that," Joe muttered.

"Darryl's no trouble. He's real good company...for a fish."

"Yeah, well...don't overdo things." He took the baby from her, jiggled the lightly wrapped bundle in his arms and said, "You mentioned coffee? Point me in the direction of the nursery and I'll put her down and join you in a cup. I could use that sandwich, too, come to think of it. You like mayo or mustard on yours? I'll make 'em."

Jeez, would you listen, he thought. Cook, butler and baby-sitter, all rolled into one. He blamed the woman. She had no business treating him as if he were a life-long friend. He wasn't. He was a man with a mission, one that wasn't going to endear him to her once he got down to brass tacks.

She reached up and set the can of fish food on a shelf, throwing her prominent bosom into even more prominence. Joe tried not to stare, but it wasn't easy. He felt a crazy combination of lust and protectiveness streak through him, gone almost before he was aware of it. It wasn't a feeling he welcomed.

Hell, it wasn't even anything he recognized.

The baby hiccuped, reminding him of his mission, and he turned away, grateful for the distraction. "Listen, Fatcheeks, I need to talk to your mama, so be a good girl and give us a break, will you?"

The nursery was a nice shade of yellow, not too pale, not too brash. The white crib was obviously secondhand, but in good condition. There was a table, a chest of drawers and a lopsided wicker rocking chair, all painted white. She'd done a nice job of building her nest, he'd hand her that, especially if she'd had it all to do alone.

She was right behind him. "What do you think?"

He said it was nice, because she obviously expected it. One thing he'd noticed about her—she soaked up compliments the way a bone-dry field soaked up rain. As if she hadn't heard too many.

"Is she wet? Do I need to change her? I'm not sure when I need to feed her again, but the nurse wrote down some instructions, and—"

"Sophie. Slow down." She was twisting her hands. "She'll let you know, all right? When she needs changing or wants to nurse, she'll let you know. Babies have a way of communicating these things.'' At least he hoped they did. "Now, come on into the kitchen and settle down while I make us some lunch.''

She looked kind of embarrassed when he mentioned nursing. As if he'd never seen a woman's breasts before. Not hers, but hell, he was pushing forty and she was no spring chicken, herself. Judging her now, he figured her for about thirty-five, but he could be off a few years. She had a mature body—a body some man had done more than just look at. There was something about her face, though, about the way she looked at him, with those big, guileless gray eyes, that made him want to forget the damned jade.

But he'd promised Miss Emma. Sooner or later he was going to have to bring up the Ch'ien Lung, and the longer he put it off, the tougher it was going to be.

Damn Donna! He'd gone easy on her that day she'd called him because she'd been crying so hard he could barely make out what she was saying. And because he'd always been a sucker for his sisters' tears. They were his baby sisters, after all. They'd gone through a lot together, even though they weren't all that close anymore.

The arrangements had all been made. The museum had offered to send somebody after the stuff, but Donna had wanted to keep it over the weekend before she took it in to be photographed for the catalog. They had an old set of photographs, but they were pretty dog-eared and the quality wasn't too great.

As it turned out, Donna had actually wanted to show the stuff off to a man she'd been seeing, who'd expressed an interest. An antique broker by the name of Rafael Davis.

According to her story, he'd waited for her to fall asleep—which was the first Joe knew that his sister had a new live-in lover—and then he'd cleaned her out and skipped town.

She hadn't discovered the theft until morning. Then, instead of calling the cops to report it, she'd called Joe. Brother Joe, ex-cop, who had bailed her out of trouble more than a few times. The jerk had done a job on her. Missing were two expensive cameras, a diamond-and-emerald ring, Miss Emma's jade collection and Rafael Davis, alias Richard Donaldson, alias David Raferty.

Twenty years ago, maybe even ten, the creep might've gotten away with it, but communications were too good these days. Even the smallest departments were coming on-line. That was how Joe had found out about the woman in Amarillo, who'd signed over her life's savings to a securities broker named Rick Donaldson, thinking he was going to invest it for their future. Instead he'd walked off with her money and a small Andrew Wyeth watercolor.

In Arkansas, he'd bilked a widow out of her late husband's insurance money, claiming he'd invested it in a house for them to live in after they were married. He'd taken her three-karat wedding ring out to be cleaned and remounted for her, and that was the last time she'd seen him.

All Joe could figure was that either women were criminally dense, or the guy was incredibly good. Or both. Donna had two college degrees and was working on her third, not to mention a lot of experience with men, all of it bad. Every time one of her marriages broke up, she swore off men, but it never lasted. She'd been fleeced just like all the rest.

He and Sophie ate in the kitchen, which suited Joe just fine. He needed a cozy, casual atmosphere to put her off guard. He planned to work his way around to the subject, even though he'd half decided to put off the hard questions until tomorrow.

"Salt?" she asked, and he shook his head.

"I shouldn't. It makes my ankles swell, but just this once I'm going to celebrate. I might even make some chocolate pudding. Did you know that nursing mothers can take in a lot more calories and not gain weight?"

He murmured a response while he framed his first question. "Sophie, do you know what a fence is?"

Her gray-green eyes widened. "Certainly I know what a fence is. You're not going to tell me I need a security fence, are you? Because I can't afford—"

"Not that kind of fence. The kind I'm talking about is—"

"Picket. There used to be one out front, but it fell down. I cleaned up the last few sections after I moved in. I'm saving them to use on a play yard."

Joe reached down and massaged his bad knee under the table. "I'm an ex-cop, not a landscape artist. A fence is street slang for a receiver of stolen goods."

"I knew that. But why—? Oh. This is about Rafe, isn't it? I was afraid of that."

She was *afraid?* Now, that was interesting. "Rafe Davis. Is that what he called himself when you two hooked up?"

She bridled at that, and he warned himself to slow down. He had plenty of time. As much time as he needed. She wasn't going to sell anything, not while he was here to prevent it. And she wasn't going to wiggle off the hook, either, because he had her right where he wanted her.

A fleeting image of a long, golden body stretched out in a rumpled bed, golden hair in a tangle over the pillow, and a pair of Spanish-moss–colored eyes gazing up at him all soft and unfocused, flickered across his mind and was quickly snuffed out.

"Rafe and I...we were...well, I'm not exactly proud—"

That was as far as she got. From the room at the end of the hall came the baby's cry. Sophie nearly tipped over her chair racing from the room, with Joe one step behind her.

Dammit, man, you were that close!

They never got back to it. By the time Iris had nursed, cried, belched, cried some more and gone through three sets of drawers, her mama was practically in tears. "Do you think she wets too much? How will I know when she's had enough to eat? Nobody ever told me that nursing would hurt, but I think I might be getting blisters. Do you think that's possible?

The nurse said I should—well, anyway, it'll probably be all right once I get the hang of it.''

Joe was slightly embarrassed, and from the looks of her, so was she. He didn't have any answers, but the longer he hung around, the more questions he was piling up. Such as why any man who prided himself on being halfway civilized would look at a brand-new mother and think the salacious thoughts he'd been thinking.

Sophie and her baby settled into the wicker rocker, the baby howling, Sophie singing snatches of something that was mostly *la-la-la* and a few *dum-dums*. She looked harried and helpless, and Joe, who had never been known as a pushover, didn't have the heart to push her about the jade again.

Tomorrow, he promised himself. Tomorrow he'd get to the bottom of the matter, take whatever she had left and leave her to get on with her life. He had a life of his own he'd walked out on, one that was still pretty much up in the air. A guy didn't just end a career that spanned half a lifetime and walk away without leaving a few crater-size gaps. He was still at the restless stage, trying to make a definite decision about whether or not to go ahead with his plans to start a security business. To a single man pushing forty, a steady diet of hard work no longer seemed quite as attractive as it once had.

Four

"They called it downsizing, but I'm pretty sure it was more personal than that. There was some talk and all—I mean, Rafe used to hang around the bank a lot while he was waiting for me to go to lunch, and then, after all the unpleasantness came to light..."

Unpleasantness. The lady had a talent for understatement.

"Do you know how hard it is to fire anyone these days?"

Joe did. He helped himself to another slice of toast and wondered how any business could get away with firing a pregnant, single female unless she'd been caught red-handed robbing petty cash, looting the retirement fund and harassing every male in sight.

Maybe not even then. "So you were downsized. What happened next?"

"Since my rent was paid up through the end of the month, I gave notice at the apartment and started looking for another job and a place to stay. Not many people wanted to hire a woman who was going to have to take maternity leave in a few months, but I can't really blame them for that."

Neither could Joe. He blamed the bastard who'd gotten her in this fix and walked out on her. If it was Davis, he was already beyond the reach of the law. If it was some other lowlife, he ought to be strung up for crow bait. But that wasn't what he'd come back to accomplish today. "So how come you sprung for a house instead of renting a couple of rooms? Isn't that a pretty big commitment for a single woman with no visible means of support?"

Loaded question. He waited for an answer. Her eyes had a way of going slightly out of focus when she was concentrating. He'd noticed it before. He'd picked up on a lot of things about her in the brief time he'd known her, which, in terms of all they'd shared, was a hell of a lot more than just a chronological few days.

"As it happened, I came into some money. I know this real estate agent—she lived in the apartment across the hall? Anyway, she told me all about this house she had listed that I could lease with an option to buy, and about equity. It's not like pouring rent money down a hole with nothing to show for it. Owning a house is an investment for the future, and besides, living in the country is cheaper than living in town.''

Smart agent. Joe wondered if she'd happened to mention incidentals like property taxes, insurance and the cost of a new roof. He'd already discovered the reason none of the second floor rooms were being used. "Yeah, sure," he said, but instead of picking up on his sarcasm she went on to detail her plans for a garden and a freezer and raising chickens. He had a feeling those plans of hers were about all she had to hang on to, which was why she liked to talk about them.

Before he could work the conversation back around to the money she'd "happened to come into," they heard what Joe was coming to think of as "the call of the wild." Three walls away and she could tell when the baby's breathing rate changed.

She'd already started selling off the jade. Severance pay would be a month's salary, at best. Hardly enough for a lease and an option, even on a down-at-the-heels fixer-upper like this.

It had to be the jade. How much of the collection had she already sold? More to the point, how the hell was he going to get it back? Repossess her house? Hell, it wasn't even hers yet.

Hardening himself for what he had to do, Joe finished his coffee, clasped both hands over his head and stretched, then carried his dishes to the sink. He listened to the small, homey sounds coming from the nursery down the hall. Mama noises. Baby noises. The sound of a drawer opening and closing. He'd deliberately refrained from joining her at feeding time. There was a limit to the intimacies a man and a woman who were practically strangers should share.

To keep him on course, he went out to the truck and placed a call to his grandmother. He'd thought about waiting until he had something concrete to report, but he worried about her. Physically, she'd recovered pretty well from the small stroke she'd had last winter. Mentally Miss Emma still had a ways to go.

"Hi, sweetheart, did I interrupt anything important?"

"I was just lying down. Are you on your way home? Did you find it?"

"I found it all right, but there's a slight hitch."

She said, "Oh." Just that. It wasn't like his grandmother not to be interested in everything that went on around her. The last time he'd called, Donna had said she was sleeping half the day. Missing church. According to his sister, the elderly were prone to depression.

Joe didn't know about that, but he did know his grandmother. She might be eighty-three on the outside, but inside, Miss Emma was ageless. There was only one woman in the world who'd ever been able to crack his shell and touch him where he lived. His mother had never done it. She'd been too busy making life hell for his dad. His ex-wife, Leeza, hadn't even tried.

He'd never been a match for his grandmother, though. Miss Emma had had his number right from the start, when he'd gone to live with her, a chip the size of a redwood stump on both shoulders.

"The baby takes up a lot of time right now. Trying to teach her the difference between night and day—you know how it is."

"I only had the one. Your father. It doesn't look like any of his offspring are going to do their duty by the family."

Joe started sweating, and it wasn't entirely the heat. Pressure did that to a man. "Look, why don't you call the museum and tell them we're back on schedule again, give or take a couple of pieces. I'll let you know as soon as I find out which ones are gone."

He almost hoped she'd kick up a fuss about it, but she didn't say a word. She'd been looking forward for nearly a year to seeing the collection installed at the museum with a placard reading, Collection of Jonathan Joseph Dana. Now she'd even lost interest in that.

The crazy thing was that he could still remember all the grief she'd given the old guy over that same collection while he was alive. "Why can't you take up fly-fishing or womanizing like any normal, reasonable man?" she'd demanded the time he'd blown eighty grand for a chunky little jadeite tray. Jonathan had launched into one of his rambling discourses about dynasties and legends until Miss Emma had whacked him down to size again. It was Dana oil money he was spending, after all, not that that had cut any ice with Miss Emma. For ninety-eight pounds of blue-haired old lady, she packed a pretty mean wallop.

Feeling older than the hills himself, Joe stared down

at the phone in his hand and thought about the two most influential people in his life. Whatever he'd amounted to, he owed it to his grandparents. They'd taken over after his parents had been killed back when Joe was eleven, Donna two and Daisy three years old. His parents had been on the verge of a long overdue divorce at the time.

Now, some twenty-seven years later, Daisy was in the process of splitting up with her third husband. Donna, also between husbands, was currently on the wagon, but she was studying too hard and driving Miss Emma crazy.

Joe had gone through a career, a marriage and his own battle with the bottle. Through it all, there'd been one constant in his life. His grandmother. Miss Emma. Jonnie—Joe's sisters had called him Grandjonnie— had been there, too. It was Miss Emma, though, who had been the North Star, the gyroscope that had held them all on course until one by one, they'd left the fold and gone out into the world to screw up their lives.

Joe sighed. His knee hurt. According to the last weather report he'd heard, there was a line of squalls headed this way, the leading edge of a tropical depression. He wasn't looking forward to it. He ached in wet weather.

So he went back inside, tiptoed down the hall to the nursery and looked in. Sophie was rocking the baby, her eyes closed, her head tilted back on a pillow she'd stuffed behind her neck.

He was tempted to scoop them both up and carry

them to bed, and if that wasn't enough to scare the hell out of a single guy who'd sworn off women in all but the most temporary circumstances, he didn't know what was.

Back in the kitchen he opened one cabinet after another, glancing at the contents and then shutting the door. The broom closet offered no more than a ragbag, an ironing board and a collection of cleaning equipment. He frisked the ragbag and felt like a fool for doing it. Not that he'd expected to find anything there, but with women, you never could tell. He'd talked to one woman who'd had a diamond necklace stolen from a toilet tissue roller.

"Did you ever think of putting it in the safe?" he'd asked her.

"But that's the first place a robber would look," she'd said, as if amazed at his naiveté.

She had a point.

Sophie called out from down the hall. "Joe, would you bring me a wet towel from the bathroom?"

"Sure, hang on."

First he had to find a towel. Then he had to wet it. Then he had to brace himself to walk in there again where she was waiting. His boots made a gritty sound on the bare hall floor as he retraced his steps. Holding a hand under the wet towel to keep it from dripping, he shouldered open the door and stood there. She was still right where he'd left her, seated in the rocker with Iris asleep at her breast. For the sake of modesty, she'd draped a crib sheet over herself, but it would take more than a square yard of rabbit-printed flannel to dull the image that etched itself permanently on his mind in that single moment.

Pale golden hair backlighted by the early-morning sun. Shadowy, translucent eyelids. Thick, pale lashes fanned out over her cheeks. Golden skin. Firm arms, long legs, soft, smooth throat. A face that was...

That was beginning to appeal to him a little too much.

Joe cleared his throat. Her eyes flashed open. "Oh. Was I dozing again? I didn't get much sleep last night."

Joe had suspected as much. He'd gone back to the hotel, packed his gear and showed up before the sun was even up, waiting on the front porch swing until he'd heard her stirring.

"Would you mind mopping off my back? I must be doing something wrong. This is the second time she's spit up all over me today, and the day's hardly even started yet. I thought mothers' milk was supposed to be so digestible."

He stared at her—at the flush on her cheeks, the way her robe drooped lower on one shoulder. The room smelled like baby powder and cottage cheese, hardly a fragrance designed to trigger lust. Which made Joe wonder if seeing her like this—with the baby and all—could have tapped into some latent reproductive instinct that had been buried inside him all these years. If Miss Emma ever found out, she'd be on him like rust on a barbed wire fence.

"Joe?"

"Yeah. Where do you want it?"

"Here, then you hold her while I mop up, will you?" She stood and tugged her robe up again and handed him the baby. "The book says if I keep her awake for longer stretches during the day she'll sleep longer at night, but it sounds so heartless."

"All new babies have the same trouble. She'll get it sorted out after a while." As if he knew. As if he was any expert on the care and feeding of infants. For all the five husbands they'd had between them, neither of his sisters had ever had a baby. It went without saying that he hadn't, either. He'd pulled a few hair-raising stunts in his life, but to his knowledge, he'd never fathered a child. Been damned careful not to, in fact.

Gazing down at the small bundle of red-faced humanity that blinked up at him so solemnly, Joe felt his insides give a crazy lurch. He put it down to the pizza he'd eaten for breakfast.

"She's looking better today," he said.

Sophie scrubbed her shoulder and adjusted the front of her robe. "What do you mean, she's looking better today? What was wrong with the way she looked yesterday?"

"Come on, Sophie, you have to admit her face was sort of lumpy and swollen. Hey, she has blue eyes, did you notice?"

"Certainly I noticed. I noticed everything about her, and anyway, all babies start out with blue eyes. That doesn't mean they'll stay that way. And her face wasn't lumpy, it was just puffy."

"Oh. Yeah, now that you mention it, I can see the difference."

She rolled up the soiled towel and dropped it onto the pile of crib sheets to be washed. She might as well add her housecoat. Sour milk wasn't going to improve with age. "I'm going to wash a load of things as soon as I get dressed. That sun had better hang in there a few more hours."

He was cradling the baby in the crook of his arm. She blinked up at him like a little owl and Sophie, seeing them like that, thought it was about the sweetest thing she'd ever seen. A rugged, intensely masculine man like Joe Dana, wearing jeans, boots and a rumpled khaki shirt, holding a newborn baby girl.

He glanced up, his dark eyes hooded. "You think you ought to be doing laundry this soon? I mean, aren't women supposed to take it easy for a few days?"

"Lovely idea. Not very practical."

"I know how to use a washing machine."

"I can't afford you. Housekeepers are a luxury I'd just as soon not get used to having."

"Maybe you'll come into some more money." He lifted an eyebrow, turning it into a question.

"I certainly intend to, but it's already earmarked for other things."

"Maybe you'll have enough left over to buy yourself a dryer."

"And maybe I'll have enough left over to get my car out of hock."

"I forgot about your car. What'll you do if you have to go somewhere in a hurry?"

As if she hadn't lain awake for hours last night, thinking about just such an emergency. Thinking about how much she didn't know about newborn infants, and how many things could go wrong way out here in the country, with no one close enough to turn to for advice. Thinking about guardian angels and wondering if they ever came in the form of rugged ex-cops from Texas, with rare smiles that could undermine a woman's best intentions if she wasn't careful.

"Joe," she said softly. "What in the world are you doing here, anyway? You came to ask me something, and you've been here, what—two days now? Three? How long does it take to ask a simple question?"

Iris was asleep, and Joe wasn't about to risk waking her up again. She was dry and happy at the moment, but he sensed it was strictly a temporary condition. Knowing he needed to take advantage of it while it lasted, he settled her in her crib, pulled the sheet up over her, his hand lingering on the small, warm body. And something came over him. Something he hadn't felt in so long he barely recognized it.

Fortunately he recognized it in time to cut it off. The feeling of tenderness. This crazy hopeless, helpless feeling that could get a guy in major trouble if he didn't watch his step.

"Right," he said, crossing his arms defensively over his chest. "I was about to ask you a couple of questions, and you were about to give me some straight answers when we got sidetracked by little Miss Fatcheeks here.''

"Just let me change into something dry and put a load in to wash and I'll join you in the kitchen. Then you can ask me anything you want to, and I promise I'll do my best to answer. I have a feeling I already know what it's about.''

She did?

Well, sure she did. If she was guilty. The jury was still out on that one. She'd placed an ad in *The Antique and Artifact Trader*, and anyone who knew anything at all about computers, which she did, knew that word was bound to get around. A smart fence had a list of private buyers. A smart fence put nothing in writing and definitely nothing on the Net.

But then, maybe she wasn't all that smart. Or maybe Davis had been smarter. Donna had fallen for the guy, and Donna was supposed to be the brainy Dana.

Ten minutes later Joe watched her move around the kitchen, putting the coffeepot on to reheat, setting out cups and a plate of chocolate doughnuts. He liked to watch her move. She moved as if she hadn't quite got back her balance after shedding all that weight. Even now she wasn't exactly what you'd call sylphlike, not like the third-string ballerina he'd had a fling with his freshman year at the University of Texas. Sophie had her own style of grace. For lack of a better word, he called it womanly.

"By the way, someone's been messing around in my bedroom closet," she said. "I always space my things a certain way to keep them from crushing. Was it you?''

He'd made a fast search of her closet, her dresser, a bookshelf and her hard drive while she was in labor, before they'd left for the hospital. Now he was embarrassed. "Yeah, it was me."

"Did you find what you were looking for?"

"What I found was that you like Chopin, chocolate and crossword puzzles, that you wear a size twelve dress and a size nine shoe, and that your left foot is half a size larger than your right one." She gaped at him. "What I didn't find," he continued, "was what I was looking for. Where is it, Sophie?"

A moment ago she'd looked sleepy. Sleepy, soft and sweet. Now she looked wary, and that bothered him. It shouldn't, but it did.

"That depends on what you were looking for. Maybe if you'll tell me what it is, I can help you find it."

"I'd appreciate that. What I'm looking for is something that belongs to my grandmother, that was stolen from my sister while the Garland Museum in Fort Worth was getting set to put it on display." She looked so shocked he almost wished he hadn't brought it up, which didn't make a whole lot of sense.

"Fort Worth, *Texas?*"

"You got it."

"But...but why would you expect to find it here in my house? I've never even been to Texas."

"Sophie, don't do this. Look, we've already established your connection with Davis. Now, why don't we go ahead and clear up the rest of it?''

Under a veneer of golden tan, she went pale. The coffeepot boiled over unnoticed. ''He's dead. I don't know what else I can tell you about him. I...I didn't really know him all that well.''

''Well enough, obviously,'' he said dryly.

She plopped down in one of the white-enameled chairs, a distracted look on her face. ''I don't understand why you're asking me all these questions. I've already told the police everything I knew.''

''What made them come after you?''

''They didn't come after me, as you put it,'' she corrected, her voice taking on a distinct edge. ''They came to—well, to notify me, I suppose. About my car.''

''I'm not following. What about your car?'' Joe got up and moved the coffeepot off the burner. He switched off the stove, and in the silence of the old house, the *click-click* of cooling coils sounded too loud. The sun had gone behind a cloud, and in the utility room, the washing machine switched gears and went into overdrive.

Sophie stood and straightened the dishes in the sink. ''It was totaled. Rafe took it and left town, and then he ran it into a train. I'd reported it stolen, of course, even before I'd figured out who took it. By the time I did, I was already so mad at him, I couldn't even cry when they came to tell me he was dead.''

She looked ready to cry now. And because he no longer believed she was anything more than another innocent dupe—and because they'd gone through some pretty personal stuff, considering they were still practically strangers—and because the more he got to know her, the better he wanted to know her—Joe made the mistake of taking hold of her shoulders.

Instead of shoving him away as any sensible woman would, she made the mistake of leaning forward and resting her forehead against his shoulder.

For a smart man, Joe told himself, he was making some seriously stupid moves.

"I've got to go hang clothes," she said, her voice muffled in his shirt.

He stroked her back. She was warm and soft. She smelled like shampoo, chocolate and baby powder. "I'll do it. You take it easy," he said gruffly.

"It's going to rain."

"Sophie, listen to me."

"I don't think I want to listen, if you don't mind." She sounded as if she might be crying.

"Honey, don't cry," he said, half sorry he'd ever started this lousy business. He could at least have waited a few more days until she had her emotions back under control.

"I'm n-not crying," she sobbed. "I've already written him off. I'm going to forget I ever knew the wretch, and b-believe me, it won't happen again. I've learned my lesson."

Whatever lesson she'd learned, it didn't keep her from blubbering all over a man she didn't know from Adam. Joe made up his mind that before he left he would drill her on a few basic security measures. Such as not letting strange men into the house. Not letting them past the front door, and most definitely not letting them get this close. Didn't she have any idea what a dangerous place the world was these days?

Sophie stepped back. While Joe was fishing around in his pocket for a handkerchief, praying it was a clean one, she tore off a paper towel, blotted her eyes and blew her nose. Then she went and removed the wet laundry from the machine.

They hung clothes together—Joe carrying the heavy basket, Sophie carrying the sack of clothespins. Joe thought about Dallas, about the house where he'd grown up and the staff that had made sure there were always fresh linens on the beds, a clean outfit ready for the private school he'd attended and enough food handy to satisfy a growing boy.

Had he ever given a single thought as to how such things came to pass?

Probably not.

"It's going to rain," he said.

"I know that. Still, a little fresh air will help, and then I can hang them in the utility room. You never did finish telling me exactly what it was you were looking for, Joe. It was something about a chain link...vase?"

"Ch'ien Lung. Look, why don't I show you a picture?" He'd brought the old ones. Even a bad photograph was better than a wordy description. What could he say? The stuff was green, not very big and not even very attractive to his way of thinking.

While Sophie took the empty basket in through the

back way, Joe went around front to where he'd parked the truck and retrieved his duffel from behind the driver's seat. Sophie was seated at the kitchen table when he got back, holding the baby. "She was fussing just a little. I thought I'd keep her up for a while."

"Yeah, sure. Now I want you to examine these pictures and—"

"You should have brought in your things, and I could've washed them along with mine."

He'd been cramming his worn shirts and skivvies in on top of his clean ones. The photos were in the bottom, where they wouldn't get bent. Which meant he had to pull out everything on top. It wasn't a pretty sight. "No problem. When I run out of clean clothes I'll stop by a Laundromat."

"Yes, but—"

"Here you go. Taken together, it's called the Jonathan J. Dana Collection. Fourteen pieces in all."

Sophie looked stricken. She picked up first one photo and then another, read the labels neatly affixed to the back listing lot number, item, circa, size in centimeters and last appraised value for insurance purposes.

"Well?" He was watching her closely. There was no way in hell she could get out of it now. The piece she'd advertised in the trade rag was item number 339 all right, complete with carved tassels, dragons and lotus blossoms, all in pale green with touches of fawn.

"Well?" she said right back at him.

"Sophie, I saw your ad. That was a bad mistake, advertising it in a publication with that wide a circulation. Don't you know every police department in the country has access to information about stolen goods?''

"I didn't steal it, it was given to me." There was a proud, wounded look about her that made him wish, not for the first time, that he'd let the insurance company track it down. They had experienced investigators who could've done the job as easily as he had. Easier. They wouldn't have gotten all mixed up on a personal level.

"And you're wrong. If I made any mistake it was letting myself be taken in by a lying, cheating, thieving skunk. Believe me, it won't happen again."

"I'm glad. You've got someone else to think about now. Before I leave, I'm going to call in a locksmith and see about—"

"No."

"No what?"

"No, thank you. If I want a locksmith, I'll call one."

That wasn't what he'd meant. Dammit, he was getting royally ticked off. Didn't the woman know he could bring her up on a charge of receiving stolen goods, if not as an accessory? At the very least he could've had her hauled in for questioning. He might not have any authority in North Carolina—hell, he didn't have any authority in Texas, not anymore, but in a case like this, a word in the right place would be sufficient.

"How many pieces have you sold?" he asked tiredly.

"I don't have to tell you anything."

"Sophie, don't make me do this the hard way."

"Why should I believe you? You barge into my garden, a perfect stranger, not even from around here—" She said it as if that was the most serious crime of all. "And then you tell me you want my engagement present? Why should I—"

"Your *engagement present*?"

"Yes, my engagement present! At least, that's what I was told. And before you start in again, remember, you're the one who warned me about strangers. Well, you're a stranger, and I'm not about to give you anything just because you say it's yours. Anybody could have those pictures. You can buy pictures like that in museum gift shops."

Joe raked a hand through his hair. "Look, Sophie—"

"No, *you* look! All my life I've been a fall person. I—"

"A fall person?"

"A fall girl. Like a fall guy. The one who's always left holding the bag. I've never been clever, I wasn't cute and cuddly when I was growing up, so I wouldn't have been adopted, even if I'd been eligible. I was always the one who got caught whenever I went along with a prank. Good ol' Sophie, she's too stupid to know when to run. That's what they used to say."

Joe reached across the table and touched her arm, but she jerked it away. The baby stirred and made those smacking sounds with her gums.

"Well, good ol' Sophie finally caught on. She's nobody's chump anymore. So you can take your damned pictures and go back to Texas and...and—"

He stood up and poured two cups of coffee that had been heated, reheated and was once more lukewarm, added cream to hers and said, "Drink it."

"I don't think I ought to be drinking so much coffee while I'm nursing. It might be the caffeine that keeps Iris awake so much at night."

"We'll check it out tonight. I'll buy you some decaf."

"You won't be here tonight."

"Oh, yes, I will, and before you climb back up on your high horse, you might as well know the worst. I'm moving into that upstairs back bedroom, leaky roof or no leaky roof." He made the decision on the spot. "I'll pay you the same thing I paid for my room at the hotel. This'll be a lot more convenient, and I need a few more days' rest before I hit the road again. I won't bring up my grandfather's jade collection until you're ready to talk about it, but—"

"Aha! First you said it was your grandmother's and now you say it belongs to your grandfather. Make up your mind."

A rumble of thunder made them both look toward the window over the sink. The sky outside was purple. Tired summer leaves flipped their pale undersides as a gust of wind blew the first raindrops against the side of the house.

Sophie said, "Oh, blast."

Joe jumped up and held out a staying hand. "I'll

get 'em in, you take care of Miss Iris. She might be scared of the noise.''

He jogged outside and started snatching wet clothes off the line while rain beat down on his bare head. He might not be certifiable, but he'd be the first to admit he was well on the way.

On the other hand, he had her right where he wanted her now. On the defensive.

Right. Then, how come he felt like a lousy dog? How come he made one excuse after another not to cut through the crap, grab what he'd come for and leave? There was still enough left to make a fair showing. As for whatever pieces she'd already sold, it had made the difference between being homeless and out of work, or having a decent home to bring her baby to. Miss Emma, if she was inclined to get tough, might want to stack that up against one more boring exhibit in a dusty, hole-in-the-wall museum.

Five

Miss Iris loved the thunder. She didn't like Joe's attempts at singing—he'd only tried it twice, when Sophie was in another room, and she'd puckered up both times. But thunder, she liked. Her eyes would get big, and she'd turn her fuzzy gaze in his general direction, as if she thought the whole thing had been arranged for her entertainment. He could've sworn she smiled a time or two, but Sophie said it was just gas.

"I thought babies were supposed to be afraid of loud noises."

"People have to be taught to be afraid. I'm not going to teach her that."

"Sophie, use your brain," Joe said patiently. They were seated in the nursery—Joe had dragged a chair in there from the living room. It was either that or sit by himself, because Sophie had taken up more or less permanent residence in her baby's bedroom. By silent, mutual consent they had postponed discussion of the jade. "There's a lot of real scary stuff out there. Any kid who doesn't know that doesn't stand much of a chance."

"How many people get killed by lightning every year?"

He wrinkled his brow. "I give up—how many?"

"Not many. And most of them are playing golf. So I'll teach her not to play golf, and she'll be okay."

"Are you serious?"

"I read up on these things. Natural hazards. Do you know how many snakebite deaths there are each year?"

"So you're not going to tell her about snakes?"

"Of course I'm going to tell her about snakes. And dogs, and cats and birds and raccoons and—"

"Lady, you take the cake."

"That reminds me, isn't it about time for lunch?"

"We just had breakfast." His second of the day.

"Well, I'm starving."

All this intimacy was beginning to get under his skin. The smell of women and babies could undermine any man's defensive mechanism. First thing you know, he'd start looking around for a woman of his own. Next thing, he'd be building a nest for her to lay her eggs in. And it wasn't going to happen.

No way.

It wasn't in the books, or in the stars, or even a remote possibility.

They had tomato sandwiches, two apiece, and Joe caught himself enjoying the way she waded into hers. The lady knew what she wanted. He wondered what she'd seen in Davis. Didn't have to wonder what he'd seen in her. It was right there for all the world to see. A big, blond, slow-talking, sweet-smiling woman with openness and integrity shining out of her eyes—which was pretty damned ironic, under the circumstances.

Not to mention a body that made a man think of long nights and short fuses.

Even when she'd been twelve months pregnant, the thought had crossed his mind. Now, he had to remind himself at least a couple of times a day that he wasn't in the market for a woman, not on a temporary basis. Not on *any* basis.

It was raining hard. Too much lightning to call Miss Emma. Besides, the last few times he'd phoned, she'd sounded so damned despondent it had depressed even him, and he didn't depress easily.

Not that he was any hard-core optimist. He'd simply learned over a lot of years to hold it between the lines. Donna called it a defensive mechanism.

He called it nobody's damned business.

They sat in the nursery while the rain droned on and little Iris slept the afternoon away. Sophie wanted to wake her up to be sure she was all right, but Joe talked her out of it. He found a deck of cards in a kitchen drawer along with a tangle of jar rings, paraffin and rotten rubber bands and used them to lure her into the living room.

They sat across from each other at the coffee table,

Sophie cross-legged on the floor and Joe on the sofa. Gentlemanly or not, there were limits to the demands he could make on his body. This was one of the reasons he'd opted for early retirement and starting his own business instead of hanging on and nailing down a desk.

"It's called honeymoon bridge," he told her as he shuffled and dealt.

She wanted to know who had invented it, and why, and they played around with that for a few minutes. Laughing. Joking. Nothing crude, but just on the edge of suggestive, because she reminded him in a way of his grandmother. Miss Emma would have scoured his mouth if he'd told a blue joke in mixed company.

With all the time in the world to talk, neither of them brought up the jade.

It was a quarter of five, eastern time, when the phone rang. Joe had just checked his watch, thinking he'd wasted an entire day when he could at least have talked to his grandmother.

"Let it ring. Your machine will pick it up."

"What machine?" She was already hurrying into the hall, where the phone was. Joe reminded himself that that was another thing he'd take care of before he left. She needed a phone beside her bed.

"Oh," he heard her say with a breathless catch in her voice. "The vase? No, I haven't sold it yet."

Another blast of lightning crackled overhead. Joe moved in behind her and said, "Hang up."

"It's...well, it's sort of a cloudy emerald green,

and— Yes, I have several other pieces you could look at... Yes, I could do that.''

"Sophie, hang up the damned phone!" Joe hissed.

"It's out in the country just off 158. You go past Smith Grove community about—well, I'm not quite sure how many miles, but there's a sign on the left that says—"

Joe took the phone out of her hands and hung up for her. "Security lesson number one—don't *ever* give out your address to a stranger. Hell, don't even *speak* to a stranger! If it rings again, don't touch it, understand? If he's really interested, he'll follow up."

And when he did, Joe would make a point of letting him know the thing wasn't for sale.

"You had no right to—!"

"I have every right," he said grimly. "In the first place, it's dangerous to use a phone with lightning this close."

"I told you I'm not—"

"Then you damned well ought to be! And in the second place, that thing's not yours to sell."

She got all huffed up over that. Eyes snapping fire, or as much fire as Spanish-moss–gray eyes can generate. "It was given to me as an engagement present. Just because my fiancé was a creep—just because the wedding never took place, that doesn't mean it's not mine to keep."

"Oh, you wish you'd married him, huh?"

"I never said that."

"Iris is his, isn't she?"

"I never said that, either!" She was angry and hurt

and confused, and he told himself it damned well served her right. All the same, when the phone rang again and she reached for it, he took her by the wrists, and then he took her in his arms and held her while the thing rang seven more times and then quit.

"Sophie, Sophie," he murmured. "Give up." She sagged against him as if she were defeated, but he suspected it would take more to defeat this woman than a missed phone call. "We need to talk about this some more."

The phone started in again. He let it ring. Six times. And then he picked it up. Someone—a man's voice—said, "I know where you live. Why don't I just drive on out there tomorrow?"

"And why don't you just forget it. There's nothing here that's for sale." He hung up the phone just as the power went off with a muffled explosion. "There goes a transformer," he said.

"I know that." She sounded calm. He had to hand it to her.

"Yeah, well, maybe you do, but you obviously don't know any better than to give out directions to your house to a stranger who—"

"You mean another stranger. I didn't give you any directions, and you found me."

Joe rubbed the back of his neck. A part of him wished he'd never talked that deputy into telling him how to find Ms. Sophie Bayard. Another part couldn't imagine *not* having found her.

The storm moved off. Iris slept on. When the power came back on, Sophie went out to the garden to see what damage, if any, the hard rain had done. She came in muddy and discouraged, with scratches on her arms and only a few pods of okra and a scant handful of late blackberries to show for her troubles. After washing up, she waked the baby from a sound sleep just so she could rock her. Said it comforted her.

Joe wished she would rock him. God knows, he could do with some comforting.

She wrote ad copy for a living. He'd figured that out from what was on her hard drive and then asked her about it. It wasn't all that hard to get her started on a subject—he had a feeling she missed working with other people and living in town—but she clammed up whenever he tried to bring up the jade.

Joe could even understand why she hated to admit to the truth. Once she did, she'd lose everything, because no way was writing ad copy for a couple of newspapers and half a dozen small businesses going to pay the bills. Wait'll she got her first property tax bill. Wait'll she got her car out of hock and it gave out on her again. Wait'll she got an estimate on getting her roof repaired.

There were a hundred and one things that could go wrong. While he rinsed their few supper dishes and stacked them in the drainer, Joe went over just a few. He didn't see any way around it. He was going to have to kick the legs out from under her, and he'd sooner break both his arms than have to do it.

But he couldn't go back empty-handed and lie to Miss Emma. Nor could he tell her he'd found the stuff, but didn't want to take it from the woman who had it, on account of she needed it to live on, while all his family wanted to do was stick it in a small museum that was open only three days a week and drew only a few thousand visitors a year.

He went around the barn a time or two on that one. In the end, he set it aside to deal with tomorrow. Something would occur to him by then.

The real mystery was why the jerk had left it behind in the first place.

It had been a long day, what with the storm and the phone call and all. Iris was fussier than usual this evening. No matter what Sophie claimed, Joe figured all newborn creatures had to have been programmed to be afraid of a few basic threats, or else how had the species managed to survive?

He dried his hands and went in to check on Sophie before he turned in. They were both there in the rocking chair. Sophie's eyes were closed. She had tipped the chair back so that Iris couldn't possibly fall out of her arms. Joe stood and watched from the doorway, thinking she looked tired. Maybe this childbirth thing had a delayed effect. She'd already lost most of that golden, sun-kissed look he'd noticed the day he'd first seen her. There were shadows under her eyes. And still, there was something about her that...

Yeah. Well. Enough about that.

"Sophie?" he said quietly from the doorway. Iris was making noises as if she was hungry. Joe was surprised she'd gone unfed this long. As a rule, her mama was quick off the mark at the first little whimper.

She made a funny little puffing sound with her lips but didn't wake up. Joe crossed to her side, his boots silent on a threadbare fake Oriental carpet. "Honey, wake up, feed the baby and go to bed," he said. It struck him that for a single man who intended to stay that way, he was beginning to sound dangerously domestic. Downright paternal, in fact.

And then he heard something else. Something that slammed him in the belly like an iron fist.

Sophie whimpered in her sleep, and Joe groaned. He touched her lightly on the arm and then shook her gently, just enough to rouse her.

Her eyes flew open, and in that split second before she came wide-awake, she was totally vulnerable.

In that moment Joe knew that he could no more walk out and leave her—leave her and her baby, with or without the jade—than he could fly to the moon. That was bad enough. What was worse was having to admit that he could be turned on by a woman who had just given birth to another man's baby. Either he was totally depraved, or the human instinct for survival and reproduction was a hell of a lot stronger than he'd suspected.

Later that night, when he was lying awake under a leaky roof, in a bed that was obviously a relic of the ark and still damp, Joe tried to figure it out. The way Sophie affected him. If a woman could experience a delayed reaction after childbirth, couldn't a man have a delayed reaction after being forced to resign from a career that had claimed his life from the time he'd graduated from college at the age of twenty-two? In both cases, there was a sudden drastic change in lifestyle and priorities.

Joe had gone into police work full of enthusiasm, determination and idealism. Some sixteen years later, with a broken marriage behind him, having survived an explosion that had left his hearing impaired, two wrecks that hadn't done his carcass any good, and a few doses of lead poisoning, he'd resigned. It was either that or hold down a desk job. He hadn't left the force a broken man, nor even a bitter one. What he had been—still was—was a devout realist.

So why, he wondered now, staring up at the ceiling in the small hours of the morning, was this particular realist spending so much time devising ways to shore up the income of a woman he'd never even met until a few days ago? What difference did it make to him if her roof ever got patched? Or if she had her locks changed or not, and an extra phone installed, and maybe a dog? A bullmastiff, something that looked fierce, but wasn't. Any kind of a dog would be more protection than a pop-eyed goldfish with an overgrown tail.

Joe thought about all this before he fell asleep, but his last waking thought was about none of the above. A soft-focused image of Sophie formed in his mind. Sophie with her breasts bare, nursing her baby. Sophie smiling up at him, sharing the moment.

Sophie, sharing all that warmth and sweetness with a beat-up ex-cop from Dallas. A man who'd tracked her down with the full intention of accusing her of a crime.

It was 6:37 the following morning when the phone rang. Joe, groggy, but with a germ of an idea of how to solve both their problems, opened one eye and squinted at his wrist. His watch was on the dresser across the room, so he lay there and swore for a few minutes, and then he eased out of bed, favoring his stiff knee, pulled up a pair of jeans and headed for the phone.

It stopped ringing before he got halfway down the stairs.

Sophie poked her head out of her door and said, "Did you hear the phone ringing?"

"Yeah. Probably a wrong number." But he didn't think so, not for a minute.

"It might be that man about the ad."

"Nah—more like a wrong number. Go back to bed, if it rings again, I'll get it."

She was wearing a nightgown, something loose and thick, with about as much style as your average feed sack. On her it looked good. She lingered in the doorway, and he waited for her to say what was on her mind. He had a feeling she still resented the way he'd handled the call last night.

"Joe…would you come feel Iris's skin?"

Would he *what?*

"She feels hot to me."

"Babies have a higher metabolism. I'm pretty sure I read that somewhere."

"But she's been fussier than usual, too. Last night she slept in such teeny-weeny little snatches. Just see what you think, will you? Maybe it's all my imagination."

Joe had the same training all big-city cops had, plus a lot of experience. He'd delivered a few babies, driven more than a few to emergency rooms, but diagnosing baby ailments was a little out of his line. He was about to say so when he saw her lower lip tremble.

Hell, he would've checked a shark for tonsillitis before he'd make her cry. "Yeah, sure," he said gruffly, and followed her into the yellow nursery.

The baby looked flushed to him, but then, she'd been born looking red enough to be purple. He laid a hand on her thigh, the width of his palm covering more than the distance to her fat little knee. And then he placed two fingers in the crease of her neck.

"She's warm, all right."

"She's hot. She's got a fever. I knew it, something's wrong," Sophie whispered. She was wringing her hands. Joe had been around her long enough by now to know she wasn't a natural-born hand-wringer.

"Calm down," he said, his mind racing over the possibilities. They hadn't been around anybody to catch anything, unless she'd picked up something in the hospital. That wasn't out of the realm of possibility. There was no question of spoiled milk, because she took hers straight from the motherlode.

"I'm going to call the doctor."

Iris was whimpering. Not howling, the way she

would if a pin was sticking her. As far as Joe knew, babies didn't even wear pins anymore. "Why don't I drive you in and let someone take a look? That'll be better than trying to diagnose over the phone."

"Oh, would you?" The relief in her eyes got to him. "Or maybe we should call an ambulance," she said, clouding up again.

"Two-way trip takes too long. I know the way now. This time of morning on a weekend there won't be much traffic. We'll call on the way and have someone standing by."

Joe laid the baby back in her crib. She was hot, all right. And listless. It didn't look good, any way you sliced it. He raced upstairs and grabbed a shirt, ramming his arms into the sleeves while he hopped around, trying to step into his boots without taking time to put on socks.

He'd ordered Sophie to get dressed and left her shedding her nightgown as if she'd never heard of modesty. Which was a pretty good indication, if he'd needed any, that he was perverted and she wasn't.

Traffic was light, which was a good thing, because before they even reached the county line the situation had worsened. When Sophie reached for one of Joe's hands and placed it on Iris's bare back, he swore—and maybe prayed a little. She was a furnace. Her temperature, if he was any judge, was already dangerously high. Joe cursed the time he'd wasted getting dressed.

He reported in halfway to town. "She's what—four days old now? Five? Maybe ten pounds or so... No problems up till now, no contacts, no—what? She's breast-fed." He glanced at Sophie. "Diarrhea?"

She shook her head, and he replied, "Don't think so. She seemed all right last night, but she's burning up now, and listless. We should be there in about three, four minutes, tops."

Sophie bore up like a trooper. She'd gotten that lioness look about her now. Nothing was going to happen to *her* cub, not while she still had breath in her body.

By the time they pulled up at the Emergency entrance she'd lost the last vestige of color in her face, but her voice and hands were steady. She handed her baby out to the white-suited attendants, slid down off the high seat and hurried after them while Joe wheeled crookedly into the closest parking space.

Inside, he ran slam into a stone wall. There'd been a time when his badge would have opened doors for him. Now all he had was attitude, and with some people, including the woman behind the desk, that only made things worse.

"If you'll just take a seat in the waiting area, Mr.—"

"Dana. I'll take a seat, but first I want to know where—"

"Are you family?"

He was tempted to say yes, but by now he knew the pitfalls. "A close family friend. The closest. I brought them in. Hell, I practically delivered her—"

"There's no use in swearing, Mr. Donner."

"Dana. Will you make sure Ms. Bayard knows I'm here?"

"Does she have insurance?"

Joe was ready for that, because he'd been the route when he'd brought her in before. He didn't have her card, though. "She delivered here. She'll be in your computer." He gave out the statistics and then stalked over to the waiting area, where he blew out his worry and frustration in a single hard gust. He hadn't taken time to shave. Hadn't taken time to wash the sleep out of his eyes, so he found a men's room and did the best he could, glancing at his watch every few minutes.

They ought to know something by now. Dammit, Sophie didn't need this! He'd give anything in the world to be back home fixing her breakfast while she rocked and nursed and sang crazy songs she made up on the spot. About fish named Darryl. About rabbits that ate chocolate-covered cherries, spat out the seeds, which promptly sprouted and produced more chocolate-covered-cherry trees.

Back in the waiting area he paced, glancing up whenever he heard footsteps. Which was a lot of glancing. Emergency rooms were noisy places by their very nature, even in a small hospital on a quiet Sunday morning.

He thought some more about the plan that had occurred to him sometime during the night. There'd been no time to mention it yet, but with any luck at all he could be back home in Dallas by the middle of the week, his mission accomplished, with no untidy ends left dangling.

"Joe? They told me you were here."

He twisted around and nearly fell when his knee clicked out on him. Sophie reached for him, he reached for her, and they stood there holding on to each other. He didn't know who was supporting whom, but it felt good. It felt damn good.

"Is she—" He couldn't bring himself to ask. If anything happened to that baby—he'd practically delivered her. That gave him a few proprietary rights, didn't it?

Sophie shuddered but she wasn't crying. "They've iced her down."

"For the fever?"

She murmured something into his neck. It sounded like "Mmm-hmm," but the way the vibrations shot through him, it felt more like a cattle prod.

"Do they know what caused it yet? Is it serious? My partner's kids used to run high fevers over the least little thing. The next day they'd be out playing ball again. Maybe she's cutting teeth." He thought about all the germs that ran rampant in hospitals. All the genetic problems she might've been born with, that there hadn't been time to check out.

"It was a tick."

"A...*tick?*"

"And it's all my fault." She did sob then, once or twice. Joe held her close and stroked her back and there-there'd her a time or two.

"Honey, it couldn't be your fault. I've never seen a more devoted mother than you are."

"I went out yesterday after the rain, remember? And I didn't change clothes before I picked her up. I must've brought it in."

Still hanging on to him, she drew in a great, shuddering breath. He patted and stroked some more, hoping she didn't realize what all this closeness was doing to him. It was way out of line, but admitting it didn't solve the problem.

"There now...I know what's wrong with you. Why don't we have some—well, whatever the machines can provide. We haven't had breakfast yet. You'll be able to think a whole lot better on a full stomach." And he'd be able to think a whole lot better with all that sweet softness across the table from him.

Or across the country.

She said she couldn't eat a bite, but Joe set her aside and strode off in search of food. Not to mention a little self-control. It was downright embarrassing to be so turned on by a woman under these circumstances. He was ashamed of himself. The last time he could remember being this ashamed of himself had been when he'd been about five. He'd gotten caught short and had relieved himself in a tennis trophy in his grandfather's library.

They ate cheese crackers, peanuts, oatmeal cookies and drank weak coffee with whitener that tasted like scented talcum powder. Sophie ate more than her share, but every few minutes she jumped up and rushed down the hall to see if there was any change.

"They ran me off," she said plaintively after the third time. "They were nice about it, but all the same—"

"Is she still here in Emergency?"

"They've taken her up to Pediatrics. The doctor's with her now. They got the tick out, but they want to keep her in here overnight. That's what I came down to tell you."

Joe thought that was a pretty good idea, what with the possibility of Rocky Mountain spotted fever and Lyme disease, but he didn't say so. No point in adding to her worries.

"She's in excellent hands. They know what to do," he said.

"I know. So you can go on back, if you want to. Naturally I'll be staying."

"Honey, all mothers want to stay with their young'uns, but if all of 'em did, they'd just get in the way."

"I won't get in the way. I'll stay out in the waiting room. I'd never be able to sleep anyway."

"Let me take you home. I can have you back here in twenty-five minutes, anytime you want to come back."

"I'm staying."

He couldn't argue. If that was his kid in there, he'd feel the same way. Did, in fact. "Did you feed Darryl?"

"Not since last night."

"Then why don't I go back, feed him and get whatever you need and come back?"

She leaned her forehead against his shoulder in that way she had, and Joe's arms went around her as naturally as if he had every right. He left her there a few minutes later, promising to be back within an hour. Knowing he was going to pass up a great opportunity to search for whatever was left of the jade.

Six

Joe turned off 158, going over in his mind what needed doing before he raced back to the hospital. He had a list. Sophie had folded it several times and stuck it into his pocket. She'd reminded him to feed Darryl, to be sure the window in the pantry was shut and that the wire fence around her garden that was supposed to keep out vegetarian predators, but didn't, was secure.

Joe reminded himself to call Miss Emma and Donna. It would take only a few minutes, and his grandmother had actually asked a question about Iris the last time he'd called her. Which was more than she'd done about the collection.

While he was at it, he'd shower and shave, and

change into a clean shirt and his last clean pair of jeans. He might even take another look around for—

No, he wouldn't. He'd made up his mind about that. He was going to tell her there was a reward, and then she'd hand over the jade and he'd hand over a few grand—he'd never touched his trust fund. Never needed it, but his pension didn't run to five-grand rewards. Besides, he'd already allocated the trust as start-up capital. With all the problems inherent in the security business, it was going to be damned expensive.

After that, he'd go back home. The museum would get the jade. Old Jonnie would get his name on a plaque. Miss Emma would dust off her hands and say, "Well…that's that," and everyone would live happily ever after.

Yeah, right.

Not until Joe reached out to unlock the front door did it come over him. Situation awareness. This time it took the form of goose bumps on the back of his arms and a prickly feeling that something was off-kilter.

Pressing his ear flat against the paneled door, he listened. And heard nothing. Silently he made his way to the front window and peered in, careful to keep a low profile.

And then he swore and headed for the front door. It was still locked. He unlocked it, pocketed the key and stood there, staring at the shambles before him. Scattered sofa cushions trailing their stuffing. Furniture tipped over—some of it broken. Someone had done a thorough job of trashing the place. Whoever had done the job had been mean mad, not just searching. There was a viciousness about the whole thing that made his skin crawl. Whoever it was hadn't been gone long, either, because the fish was still flapping on the floor beside his overturned aquarium.

Grim-faced, Joe stepped over a pile of books and an upturned wastebasket, scooped up the fish and took him to the kitchen. "Sorry, guy, this will have to do for now," he said, and dropped him into a soup bowl filled from the tap. He had a feeling there was more to the care and maintenance of a goldfish than that, but at the moment it was the best he could do.

All he could think of was, thank God they hadn't been here. Thank God Sophie and the baby had been out of the house!

He wished now he'd paid more attention to the voice on the phone. He'd heard only a few words, just enough to know it was male, nasal and unpleasant.

Point of entry was easy. The pantry window had been left open. The screen was knocked out. There were clods of mud on the floor. He checked the prints outside the window—there were several, all from the same pair of shoes. A size ten, about a hundred-forty pounds give or take. He recognized the distinctive imprint of a popular brand of athletic shoe, which didn't make his job a whole lot easier. Probably a third of the men in Davie County owned a pair, and a third of those were probably a size ten.

Ah, jeez, she didn't need this.

His first instinct was to go after the creep. But then

he thought about bringing Sophie home to this mess, and realized he couldn't let her see it. He wasn't sure if he could talk her into going to a hotel and wondered what possible excuse he could give. For all he knew, she might not even be coming home tomorrow. It could be the next day. Or the next.

His gut clenched at the thought of what that would mean. He'd never heard of an infant getting any of the various tick-borne diseases, but that didn't mean it couldn't happen. Less than a week old, the poor little kid wouldn't stand a chance.

The word he uttered was more prayer than curse. He felt so damned helpless. It wasn't the first time he'd felt that way, but it was a sensation few cops ever got used to.

He was standing in a mess of flour, rice and dry cereal, staring down at canisters, pots and pans. And broken dishes. As if the scumball had raked them out of the cabinets for the fun of hearing them break. A sack of dried beans had been ripped open and slung across the floor. He stood there and swore some more, but then he clamped a lid on it, took out Sophie's list, unfolded it and started to read.

From bedroom: a nursing bra and a pair of underpants, top drawer, left-hand side. Nightgown hanging on back of closet door. Slippers beside bed. Hairbrush.

From kitchen: pills from shelf beside clock. Candy bars from covered jar beside refrigerator. All of them.

From bathroom: toothbrush, toothpaste, moisturizer in pink bottle, bottom shelf. Blue box under lavatory.

He found a plastic grocery bag and scooped up the

pill bottles—two prescriptions and a vitamin supplement. The candy bars were buried under all the crap on the floor. He'd replace them on the way into town.

He then tried the bedroom. There was nothing in the top drawer, or any other drawer. The mattress had been slashed and overturned, the dresser toppled after the contents had been dumped in a pile and scattered. Joe, possessed of a kind of hard, cold anger he hadn't felt in many a year, did the best he could.

The underpants were easy. Several pairs were caught on a lampshade. He chose a pretty peach-colored pair, no lace, no fancy cut. The bras were not quite that easy. He'd never seen a nursing bra before, but he figured it must be the no-nonsense number with the flaps in front. He found a couple and tucked them into his pocket.

Going through her underwear this way, when she wasn't around, made him feel like some kind of a creep. A voyeur. Joe told himself it was no more than any husband would do for his wife under similar circumstances, only Sophie wasn't his wife.

On the other hand, in the brief time they'd known each other, he'd done a few things for her that some husbands never got to do. That gave him certain rights, didn't it? Certain privileges? At the very least, a legitimate interest?

Next he headed for the bathroom. At least her toothbrush hadn't been touched. He grabbed that and a new tube of toothpaste and the pink bottle from the medicine cabinet. The only thing under the lavatory besides drainpipes was a can of bathroom cleanser, a bowl brush and a pair of rubber gloves. The rest had been trashed. There were two blue boxes on the floor, both of them empty. One had held some kind of blue scented powder. He seemed to remember his wife using something similar in her bath, only hers had been green.

The other blue box had held another familiar feminine product, each one individually wrapped. He thought about gathering them up and cramming them in on top of the rest of the stuff, but then she'd want to know where the box was, and he wasn't ready to answer any questions.

So he swore some more and jotted down the pertinent data so he could buy her another box on his way back to the hospital. Remembering the way she'd folded the list over and over, not quite meeting his eyes, some of the grimness left his face. Bless her heart, she'd been embarrassed. He could've told her if she'd asked, that a nurse could have provided her with most of the items she needed.

"Sophie, Sophie, what am I going to do about you?" he whispered. Taking one last look around, he went out to his truck and called in on his mobile to report the break-in. Assured that someone would be out right away, he settled down to wait. He tried to remember what kind of candy bars she liked, but couldn't, so he decided to get her a big box of chocolates, instead. Might save answering questions.

Time passed. Heat simmered. Under a cloudless sky, the sun was merciless. Inside the pickup, Joe sat, thighs sprawled wide, arms crossed over his chest, his face expressionless and all the more chilling because of it. Not that he hadn't seen this kind of thing before. He had. Every cop had.

But this time it was personal. This time it had happened to Sophie. And for reasons he didn't care to explore, Joe felt as if this time it had happened to him, too.

Sophie sat by the crib, cupping a tiny foot in one hand, and gazed down at the small face. Fatcheeks, Joe called her. Sophie had been indignant the first time she'd heard it, but he was right. She did have fat cheeks. And a button nose. And a tiny, pointed chin and a curvy, little rosebud mouth no bigger than a doll's mouth. Now that her skin was pink and white instead of red, you could even see her hair—a pale, transparent fuzz that wisped up on top.

A nurse came in and took her temperature, then smiled encouragingly and left. Sophie let out the breath she hadn't even known she'd been holding. It had been almost back to normal the last time, but the doctor had said he wanted to watch for any sign of inflammation.

She was still fretful. The nurse said that was natural. Sophie knew better. She needed feeding, but so far they'd allowed her only boiled water. The doctor had said if her temperature was normal and she woke in the night, Sophie could nurse her. Meanwhile, a nurse's aid had brought in a breast pump and showed her how to use it, which was embarrassing and uncomfortable, but not as uncomfortable as painfully engorged breasts.

And through it all, Sophie alternately prayed for her baby's recovery and thought about Joe. Which made her feel ashamed, because the last thing a woman in her circumstances should be thinking about was a man. Any man. Especially a man who believed she was a crook. A man who moved in and took over her life at a time when she was in no condition to stop him.

And now she didn't even want to stop him, and that made it worse.

"Gentleman in the waiting room to see you, Ms. Bayard. He brought you some things from home. Lucky you." The aid rolled her eyes and grinned.

Sophie stood, brushed a kiss on Iris's pale fuzz and tugged at her dress. Nothing fit her anymore. Her maternity things were too large, her prematernity clothes too tight. She'd just assumed that once she'd had her baby she would go back to her old figure, which, while generous, had been firm and shapely enough. She'd always been tall and big-boned. It wasn't something dieting could change.

Now she was one big bundle of flab. She felt tired and worried and unattractive as she hurried out to the waiting area, ashamed of herself for even caring what she looked like.

"Joe, thank you. Did you find everything all right? Did you remember to feed Darryl? Oh, Lord, I forgot to tell you where I keep the fish food, didn't I?"

"On the shelf with your tapes and CDs. Sorry it took me so long. I had a few errands. How is she?"

She took the two sacks from him, one of clothes, the other of personal articles and the box of chocolates. "Oh, you shouldn't have done that," she said, ripping at the clear plastic wrapper. "Her temperature's down almost to normal. I never realized how fast something could happen to a baby. I've never been so scared in my entire life." She picked out a big dark chocolate-covered cherry, bit into it and closed her eyes. "Oh, I needed this, I really did." They were standing several feet apart, and shyly, she held out the candy box.

"No, thanks. What else do you need?"

What she needed more than anything else was to walk right up to him, lay her head on his shoulder, feel his arms close around her, and hear that deep, Texas drawl telling her everything would be all right. And that was even scarier.

"Look, I've, uh, got a few more errands, a few calls I need to make. Will you be all right here for a while? I'll come back tonight, just to see if you need anything else."

"Sure, I'm fine. I'm pretty sure we'll be able to go home in the morning, once the doctor's been by to look at her. And Joe—guess what. She recognizes my voice! All I have to do is say her name, and if she's awake, she looks right at me. That's pretty advanced for someone her age, don't you think so?"

"Remarkable," he agreed, and the austere lines of his face eased, making him look almost boyish for an instant. He was standing with his feet braced apart, his hands in front of him, left hand holding his right wrist. Sophie could picture him with a cowboy hat in his right hand and wondered if he'd ever worn one. He'd look good in a battered Stetson—a black one, with the brim curled up on the sides. He had the kind of lean, wiry physique that would look good in anything.

Or in nothing.

"Are you feeling all right?" he asked. "You look kind of feverish, yourself. Sure you don't have a tick lodged somewhere on you? I could check it out if you want me to."

She was touched by his teasing, knowing that he didn't mean anything suggestive by it. He was only trying to take her mind off her worries. Laughing, she shook her head. "I'm tired. I think I must have clenched every muscle in my body, willing Iris's temperature to go down."

And clenched a few more, recognizing what this man was coming to mean to her. She'd told herself over and over that it was a case of—what was the word, propinquity? She'd latched on to him only because he was here, and she didn't have anyone else at the moment. Not anyone close. No matter who had happened along at that particular time and done all the things Joe had done for her, it probably would have affected her the same way. Once her emotions settled down again, she'd be questioning what she'd ever seen in him.

Or maybe this was all just a part of his good-cop,

bad-cop routine, or whatever they called it on her favorite detective show.

"I still think you look a little rocky. Better get something to eat. It's early, but there's a steak house not far from here. Why don't we—"

She shook her head. "I can't leave. They said I could start nursing her again tonight if her temperature's normal, and I don't want to eat anything that might upset her."

"Okay, then I'll bring supper to you. Steak shouldn't be a problem. How do you like it, rare? Medium? You want fries or baked potato?"

"Well-done and fries," she said, feeling the first pangs of hunger she'd felt all day. "Wait. Make that a salad, instead. And no onions. And no radishes—oh, and fat-free dressing if they have it."

She looked down at her body, and Joe looked at it, too. When their eyes met again something sparked between them that had nothing to do with food or babies or even the jade they both claimed. Sophie was shocked to be feeling such a thing when she hadn't even recovered from childbirth. Women lost interest in sex after they had a baby—she'd heard it over and over.

"On second thought, I'm not really hungry."

Joe just looked at her, making her miserably aware of the limp, ill-fitting cotton she'd worn all day. She sighed. "Go home, Joe. Go do whatever it is you need to do, we'll be fine here. They look after us real well."

He left her then. She swallowed her disappointment and told herself it was just as well. He was probably relieved to be let off the hook. He certainly didn't owe her anything. Just the reverse, in fact.

She watched him all the way to the elevators, noticing things about him she had never noticed about another man. Not even Rafe. Not even the man she'd been engaged to briefly several years ago, who had broken the engagement when his company had transferred him to the West Coast. Promised her he'd call the minute he got settled, but he never had.

Joe was like a different species, which was probably why she was so fascinated by the way he was built. The way his shoulders swayed when he walked, but his hips didn't. The way he carried his hands, as if they could curl into fists at a moment's notice.

Or cradle a baby.

Or caress a woman's body...

Instead of heading back to Davie County, Joe pulled into a fast-food place, parked and called the sheriff's office to see if anyone had checked out the Bayard place yet. They hadn't. There'd been a bad wreck over near Fork, but as soon as they had a man to spare...

"Right. Look, you know my credentials. Why don't I just check the place over for evidence." He'd already given the place a quick once-over. "If I find anything, I'll bag it and save it for you. The house is a real mess. Ms. Bayard's baby's in the hospital. She'll be bringing her home first thing tomorrow, and I don't want her walking in, seeing things the way they are now."

Luckily he made a habit of checking in with the local law-enforcement agencies as soon as he hit town as a matter of professional courtesy. Not to mention the fact that it saved time in case he happened to need help.

After breaking the connection, he punched in a new set of numbers. "Hi, Granny, it's me—Joe." He waited for her standard rejoinder, which usually went a long the lines of, "Don't you granny me, you young puppy, my name is Emmaline!"

She said instead, "Oh. You're still in North Carolina, aren't you?"

So he told her about Iris's tick bite. She seemed more interested in that than in the collection. "I'm real sorry it's taking so long, but we're on the homestretch. Don't laugh, but right now I'm fixing to do some housework."

She didn't even bother to ask why. "Is she going to be all right? Your father had whooping cough when he was only a baby. I worried myself sick."

"Yeah, well…Sophie's handling it real well. She's a good mama. Did I tell you she grew up in an orphanage? She says she used to look after the younger kids. It gives her an edge."

Joe didn't know whether it did or not, but he felt the need to keep his grandmother on the line as long as he could get a response from her. Any kind of a response. Maybe he should have told her he was thinking about marrying Sophie and adopting Iris, just so she'd stop nagging him about grandchildren. Only then he'd have to come up with a good reason for changing his mind when he turned up alone.

He teased her a few minutes more, but it was rough going. Depressing. So he broke the connection, called Donna, asked several questions, fielded a few of hers and then sat there in the pickup. As he stared out across the railroad tracks at a busy highway, his mind circled high and free over his problems like an eagle riding the thermals.

Looking for perspective.

Not finding it.

Making a snap decision, he backed out, pulled into the drive-in line and ordered four hot dogs all the way, two orders of fries and two big chocolate shakes. To go. Cleanup could wait.

They ate in the solarium. There was no one else there. It was visiting hour. Everyone else was visiting.

"I can't eat all this, I'm full of candy," Sophie protested. He'd sent a nurse in after her, informing her he'd brought her a few more necessities.

"You're not going to. Half of it's mine. If it's the onions you're worried about, we'll put 'em all on my two dogs, but I'd lay odds Miss Fatcheeks is going to take to them just like her mama does."

Without even thinking, Sophie bit into a hot dog, onions and all. "What makes you think I like onions?"

"Sophie, Sophie. I know you better than you think. I took one look at you that first day and I said to myself, now there's a lady who likes her onions."

She didn't laugh—her mouth was too full—but her eyes sparkled like polished moss agates. It was progress.

They finished off everything, and Joe told himself he'd done his good deed for the day. He'd fed her. He'd made her smile. He'd taken her mind off her problems for a little while, and now he was going to go back home and clean her house.

All that was for her. The rest was for him, so he could leave here with a clear conscience. A dog. New locks. A decent alarm system. Something simple to operate and not prone to false alarms. In Dallas, about ninety-eight percent of the alarms that went off were false ones. Here, there were fewer alarms, but fewer cops to respond, too.

"Look, Sophie—" He tried to come up with a non-threatening way to broach the subject.

"Joe, I've got to go back to the room."

Maybe later, he thought as she stood and collected his trash along with hers. She smiled again. Even in her ill-fitting, rumpled dress, with her hair curling untidily around her face and a smidge of mustard on her chin, Joe thought she was the most beautiful woman he'd ever seen. And in his prime he'd been considered something of an expert on women. Attracting them had never been a problem for him.

Attracting this one was. Alarm bells were going off all over the place, and he knew he had to get out of there before he did something really dumb.

"Look, I'd better head on back out—"

"Joe, thanks for not taking me at my word. Things are so crazy here. It's like another world. I hardly know if it's breakfast time or supper time, much less how long I've been here, but—"

A man cleared his throat from the doorway. "Er, um...Detective Sergeant Dana? Sir?"

Seven

His sister Daisy always said it was a mystery to her how uniformed policemen could stay looking crisp and cool on the hottest day of the year. This one was trying hard, but he was wilting. Still creased but sweating hard, he stood at attention by the solarium doorway.

"Here," Joe replied, wishing he'd left three minutes ago. He shot a glance at Sophie, preparing himself to answer a slew of questions he wasn't yet ready to answer. What he saw on her face wasn't curiosity. It looked more like fear.

Fear? She was afraid of the law?

Oh, hell.

"I'll take care of it, Sophie. You'd better get on

back to Miss Fatcheeks. If it's about my license plates, officer—''

It was the best he could come up with at short notice. He steered the deputy over to the other side of the room and waited until Sophie left. Halfway through the doorway, she glanced over her shoulder, and he sent her what he hoped was a reassuring smile.

It didn't work. She seemed puzzled, doubtful and wary.

"What license plates?" the young deputy asked.

"Sorry. Diversionary tactic. Ms. Bayard doesn't know about her house yet. I'd just as soon keep it that way until I've had time to clean up the mess. She's got enough to worry about without that. Brand-new baby up in Pediatrics. What have you got?"

"She don't know about the break-in yet?"

"It happened sometime after I brought her in this morning."

"There was these tire tracks pulled off to one side. It didn't match none of the others. Does Ms. Bayard wear a size seven-and-a-half shoe?"

Sophie sucked the last of her chocolate shake through the straw and peered over to see if the noise had disturbed Iris. She touched the tiny brow, then tucked her fingertips into a neck crease. It was warm, but not too warm.

License plates? What was wrong with Joe's license plates, other than being almost too muddy to read?

For one awful moment she'd believed the sheriff had come about the jade. It was a mark of just how rattled she was that instead of worrying about having to give it back and then scrambling around to find another job to make ends meet, she'd been worried about Joe's leaving her.

Well, of course she would give it back. And of course he would leave. There'd be no reason for him to stay, once he got what he'd come for.

Frowning, she went over the facts—at least those she knew—in her mind. While she rehashed the whole pathetic business—how she'd come in while Rafe had the pieces spread all over the table, and how when she'd asked what it was, he'd told her it was her engagement present. Fool that she was, she hadn't even wondered why he would buy her something like that instead of a ring. As he'd mentioned collecting antiques, she'd put it down to his superior knowledge and tried to look appreciative. After he'd robbed her and left, and she'd learned how valuable it was, she'd tried to reassure herself he had come by it honestly. In her heart, though, she no longer believed it.

Did that make her an accessory after the fact? Or before it, or whatever the proper terminology was?

She was sorry she'd ever laid eyes on Rafe and his antique doodads and whatnots. Without him, she'd still be working at the bank; living in her comfortable, modern, air-conditioned apartment; going out to lunch with Terri and Jeanne and to movies and dinner once a week with Eddie Dinsmore from the downtown trust department.

And if she hadn't taken the jade to work with her he would have taken it with her other valuables. Without the jade, she wouldn't be living out here in the country now.

Probably would have been living in a shelter somewhere, in fact.

Iris whimpered in her sleep, and Sophie reached out to touch her fat little knee, wanting to pick her up, not quite daring on account of that bulldog of a nurse frowned at her every time she did.

If it weren't for Rafe, she wouldn't have Iris, she reminded herself. And if Rafe hadn't robbed all those other poor women, she would never have met Joe.

Did silver linings ever tarnish?

Joe swore softly and sank down onto the cushionless sofa, staring at the thing he'd just retrieved from the pile of broken glass, marbles and wet magazines. It had been in the damned aquarium all the time. Thirty-six grand. Lying on its side in a cheap aquarium with a fake diver, a fake treasure chest and a fake shipwreck, it had been all but invisible. Half-buried, with a coating of algae disguising the details, it would've looked like some kind of grotto if anyone had even bothered to look past the late Darryl and his magnificent tail.

He set the thing on the coffee table, algae and all. Rising from the low sofa wasn't as easy as getting down had been, but he did it anyway, grasping his thigh and grimacing. He still had the rest of the house to clean tonight. Not that he'd been able to do much to the living room. His skills didn't extend to furniture repair.

He could take the Ch'ien Lung and walk out right now. Or he could use it as leverage to get her to tell him where the rest of the stuff was. He had wondered if the thieves had found the rest of the jade and then decided they hadn't. Wanton destruction indicated frustration.

Why did things have to be so complicated? Sophie didn't need the hassle. It wasn't as if she'd taken anything herself. She might've suspected it was stolen—hell, he'd told her that, right up-front—but that didn't make her guilty of anything worth reporting, not to his way of thinking.

Granted, his way of thinking had done a one-eighty over the past few days.

But dammit, what was a pregnant woman with no family supposed to do after she'd been seduced, robbed, deserted and downsized? With a baby on the way and no one to advise her, she had let herself be talked into moving into a white elephant she couldn't afford and probably wouldn't be able to hang on to, unless she came into another fortune.

Just how much of the stuff had she sold, anyway?

Joe stood in the middle of the mess in the kitchen, rubbed the back of his neck and wished he'd never heard of Sophie Bayard and her baby. Or Rafael Davis and all his aliases. Wished his grandpa had collected raincoats or dead bugs or balls of string—anything except antique jade.

If the choice was his, he'd walk away. What difference would it make? He never went to museums, anyway.

But it wasn't his call. Miss Emma was counting on him. "Find Jonnie's jade, Joey. Bring it home," she'd said, her voice still slightly slurred. She'd looked so fragile, lying there on the big, canopied bed. "You're all I've got now."

Back when Daisy and Donna were going through men, booze and credit cards as if there was no tomorrow, and Joe's wife was going through her own brand of craziness, they had agreed privately—he and Miss Emma—that of all the Danas, they were the only two sane ones left. They'd laughed about it, although it really wasn't all that funny.

Then last fall she'd scared the devil out of all of them by suffering a stroke. One morning she sat down in the library with her second cup of tea to read the stock report, an after-breakfast ritual, and three hours later when the housekeeper had come to bring her the mail, she'd still been sitting there, her head tilted awkwardly against the wing chair. Her eyes had been open, but she'd been totally nonresponsive. The housekeeper had called 911, and the call had been relayed to Joe. He'd gotten there before the ambulance.

All the way to the hospital he'd talked to her, trying to break through. He'd been terrified that she wasn't going to make it. There wasn't enough of her to put up much of a fight. That first week he hadn't left her for more than a few hours at a time. When they took her for therapy or tests, he would race home and clean himself up, grab a bite to eat and go through the mail so he could read it to her. Reassuring himself she could hear—she could comprehend—she just couldn't respond.

He'd read her everything, even the junk mail. He'd talked about her pet charity, and how it was time to start making plans for the annual fund-raiser. Day after day he'd talked himself hoarse. The morning she'd squeezed his fingers, he had broken down and cried. Then he'd gone downtown and turned in his resignation, justifying it by telling himself he was too busted up to be much good on the force anymore.

After fourteen years with the Dallas Police Department, he'd made detective sergeant. At first he'd liked what he did, but too much was changing, too fast. Too much had already changed. Evolution was one thing—no society ever stood still—but the direction things were headed was scary. Too many crimes never got solved. Even when they did, the overall picture didn't seem to improve. After a while it had got to him. The work had become too frustrating, too corrosive, too depressing. It bred cynicism, not to mention alcoholism. Good men dropped out because they saw what was happening and knew they didn't stand a snowball's chance of changing things.

So Joe had quit police work to talk Miss Emma into coming back. Now she was back about seventy-percent physically. Her doctor said that was damned good at her age, and he felt justified. Rewarded.

They joked about it. Joe told her her backhand would probably never be the same, and she always smiled, but she didn't laugh. Never laughed anymore. She was rattling around in a house that was too big and too empty. She'd lost interest in bossing him around, lost interest in all the things that used to keep her going. Her charity work. Her family. Daisy and Donna looked in on her regularly, but neither of them was willing to move in with her. They had their own lives.

Besides, they'd have driven her nuts in no time. Miss Emma called them floozies, and they called her—behind her back, of course—Queen Victoria.

Kaleidoscopic memories flickered through his mind, and he smiled nostalgically.

March yourself right back upstairs and put on a dress, young lady!

Wash that paint off your face, you look like a hussy!

Straighten those shoulders, ladies don't slump!

She'd been too old, even then, to take on the raising of a defensive boy on the edge of adolescence and a pair of spoiled little girls. Not that it had even occurred to him until years later. He'd had his own brand of rebellion to work through.

Shaking himself free of the past, Joe located a box of trash bags, a broom and dustpan.

What he needed was a rake.

"What I need," he muttered, "is a damned torch!"

But he swept, sorted and patched up the best he could, dreading Sophie's reaction when she saw what had happened to her house.

She wouldn't fall apart. Oh, no, not Sophie. She might be a little shook up at first—who wouldn't be? But she'd hold it together. He was coming to believe there was more to Ms. Bayard than met the eye, and what met the eye was pretty damned impressive.

He called her just before the hospital switchboard shut down for the night. "How's it going? Are we clear for tomorrow?"

"Oh, Joe, she's going to be all right! She nursed a little while ago and then went right to sleep, and her temperature's back to normal."

Joe shifted the phone to the other hand, leaned against the wall and crossed his ankles. He could almost see the way Sophie would be looking right now, that shy half smile, her eyes all bright and eager, as if she wanted to share her joy with him, but wasn't sure he'd be interested. There were still a few potholes in her self-confidence. He wondered about her family. What had happened to it? What had she been like as a child?

"Great. What time shall I pick you up?"

"You don't have to—"

"Sophie, what time do you want me?"

They settled on ten o'clock, and he hung up and called Miss Emma. With the time difference, he didn't have to worry about her being asleep. She turned in early but then watched TV half the night. Claimed it helped her fall asleep. Before her stroke, she'd watched a show called "Baywatch." He'd teased her about the spandex parade. She'd come back with something about having a pool put in the back lawn, where her great-grandchildren—*if* she ever had any—could learn to swim.

Now he told her about finding the Ch'ien Lung, and

where he'd found it. He thought he caught a hint of amusement in her voice. That was a rare commodity these days.

"Smart woman. Most crooks these days are so ignorant. They don't make them like they did in my day. Why, I remember reading about this case up in Chicago..."

Her voice dwindled off. Her attention span was down to zilch. Nevertheless, Joe said he didn't believe Sophie was actually a criminal, but that she'd gotten involved with the wrong man.

"Well, in my day..."

"In your day?" he prompted. Earth to Miss Emma.

He was just about to give up and say good-night when she spoke again. "Did the baby lose weight?"

"Lose what? Oh, you mean with the fever?"

"Babies lose a few ounces right after they're born. Your father did. I told Jonnie it didn't mean anything, but he was so afraid he'd be runty, like my side of the family."

Joe grinned from ear to ear. Not only had she introduced a new topic, but she'd even elaborated on it. He felt like shouting. They talked for a minute or so about his father and how he'd shot up nine inches in his last two years in high school, and Joe told himself it was an encouraging sign. But what he wanted her interested in was the future, not the past.

On the way to the hospital the next morning he stopped by Hanes Mall and located a pet shop. They were fresh out of Darryls, but he bought the habitat, complete with all accessories, and then picked out a couple of fancy goldfish. They were pretty ugly, but at least they had long tails. And because it was so hot and he didn't know how long it would be before they got back home, he bought a cooler to hold the paper carton of fish.

On the way out, he passed a florist and picked up a bunch of mixed flowers that reminded him of Sophie. Big, sunny yellow ones with dusty gray-green foliage. For good measure, he picked out a miniature bouquet of pink rosebuds for Fatcheeks.

Then he got out of there before he could do any more damage to his wallet. He told himself it was only a diversionary tactic, to take her mind off what she was going to have to face when she got home.

He told himself it was an apology for what he was going to have to do to her.

He told himself it was the heat, but hell—he was used to heat. The temperature in Dallas had hit a hundred and six last week.

It was almost noon before they were ready to leave the hospital. The doctor had been late coming by to sign Iris's release. Sophie looked tired, but joyous, as she related the doctor's orders on the way out. "He said to watch her and report any sign of infection or irritation, and he gave me something for the itch."

Joe took the baby and the diaper bag, leaving Sophie to bring the rest. He caught an elderly couple smirking at them and scowled, wanting to tell them he wasn't half of a couple. He sure as hell wasn't a third of a trio. Wanting to tell them that these people—the woman at his side, the baby in his arms—were nothing to him. By tomorrow, he'd be on his way back to Texas with what was left of Miss Emma's collection, and Sophie could go back to digging in her garden and writing copy about clearance sales and special discounts for senior citizens.

He delayed as long as he could. He drove her to get her car. Insisted on buying lunch and her groceries, claiming he intended to eat his share and part of hers. He'd have driven her to the Ashboro Zoo if he thought she'd go along with it, but there was no way he could justify delaying much longer.

Besides, it was hot. Darryls I and II were probably floating belly-up back there in the camper. The flowers would already have wilted. The baby was starting to get fussy and he knew Sophie wasn't about to unbutton her blouse and nurse in the front seat of her car.

It was nearly three by the time they got home. He braced himself for the worst. He'd done the best he could, even poking the stuffing back inside the sofa cushions, patching it with duct tape and placing the throw pillows so the patches wouldn't show, but the place still looked like it had been through a hurricane. Any cop would know right off that it had been violated.

Before they even got inside, Iris went from fussing to four-alarm yelling. Sophie jiggled and there-there'd her. Joe couldn't help but notice the damp places on the front of her blouse.

"I'd better..." She stopped just inside the living-room doorway and stared. A frown tugged at her eyebrows, and she said, "Something's wrong. That blue chair doesn't belong over there by the window, the upholstery will fade. Where's Darryl?"

"Let's see if we can settle Iris in her crib, and then we'll talk about it."

"She's hungry. I need to feed her. Joe, what happened to my pictures?"

The pictures on the wall had been trashed, along with everything else.

"Joe?" Her eyes were large, her voice small. "What's going on?"

"I'll explain everything, but first let's get Iris settled. You give her her dinner while I bring in the stuff from the truck."

He started out but then thought better of it. She was already halfway down the hall. "Sophie, um, why not use the kitchen?"

"I'd rather— Oh, no. Not the nursery. Joe? Oh, God..."

They'd done the nursery. They'd done the whole damned house, including the upstairs rooms, none of which was even furnished except for a bed and a red-wood bench in the one he was using. His clothes had been dumped on the floor, but the only things missing were the photos. He hadn't wanted to bring it up until she'd had time to get over her initial shock, but that's what this was all about. The jade.

They sat in the kitchen, because on the surface, it showed the least damage. Other than the fact that the glasses they were using didn't match and there was a big gouge on the tabletop where the creep had thrown something down on it, it wasn't in bad shape.

"Okay, here it is," he said, pouring them both another glass of tea. Her computer was missing. So far she hadn't even noticed that. "Yesterday, while we were both at the hospital, somebody broke in here and tore things up. Now, why do you suppose anyone would do that?"

She'd already lost her tan. Now she looked gray.

"We both know what they were looking for, Sophie. I don't think they found it. And I'm not saying I blame you," he hastened to add. "Davis gave it to you, and you had no way of knowing then it had been stolen. But now you do, and you realize that somebody besides the two of us knows it's here. So what do you want to do about it? Explain to the police and let them take it in as evidence? Give it to me so I can get it back to the rightful owner? Try to hang on to it and hope to hell you're not home the next time somebody comes after it?"

She didn't say a word. Not a single word in her own defense. He wished she would. Then he might not feel so much like he was throwing stones at an unarmed woman.

"Ah, jeez, Sophie— Look, let's just handle this thing between us, can we do that? You hand over the rest of the jade—I've already found the Ch'ien Lung vase. Give me what you've got left, and I'll get the word out that it's no longer here. A couple of paragraphs in the newspaper should do it. We'll set up some protection for you—locks, an alarm system, a dog. And then—''

''No.''

''Huh?''

''No dog.''

His shoulders sagged with relief. ''Not even a small one? A little yapper?''

''I'm not having any dog.''

Joe told himself he was over the top now. The rest would be downhill. ''Okay, no dog. An attack parrot, maybe, but no dog.'' And then he broke off, raked back his chair and said, ''Oh, hell.''

She followed him down the hall to where he'd left the cooler and the rest of the gear from the pet shop. ''I'll need help with this. All I know about fish I learned from the menu in a seafood restaurant.''

Later, Joe watched while she examined everything and then scrubbed every scrubbable surface. She couldn't even work until she replaced her computer. Or the police recovered it, which was highly unlikely.

She stood in her garden for a long time, as if staring at a few scraggly rows of vegetables could steady her in an unsteady world. If it worked for her, he thought, watching from the kitchen window, he might be tempted to take up gardening himself.

There was still some sorting out to do, mostly putting pictures back in frames under new glass and books on the shelf. Placing photographs back in an old album.

While Sophie gave Iris her supper, Joe found himself studying a snapshot of a girl who could only be

Sophie at about eight, give or take a year. Tall, big-boned even then, she was not what most people would call a cute kid. Knobby knees, big teeth, she was dressed up in an outfit that had obviously been made for somebody else, squinting into the sun, a resentful expression on her face. The house behind her looked big and institutional. There were a few kids in the distance and a woman standing on the steps, arms crossed over her chest, glaring at the picture-taker. Nobody was saying cheese.

Joe felt something lurch painfully inside him. Donna and Daisy had both been small. They'd had a lousy set of parents, but one thing their mother had never done was neglect her baby girls. She would dress them in outrageously expensive clothes and then pitch a fit when they got dirty. They were given all kinds of expensive toys—usually collector dolls. The look-but-don't-touch variety.

For years Joe had listened to the late-night arguments, the accusations and cross-accusations, the threats to close charge accounts and burn credit cards. More often than not, he would get up and go to the john, shut the door and quietly throw up.

So much for wedded bliss. His parents' marriage, his own, his sisters' and maybe even his grandparents'. Some men didn't have it in them to make a woman happy. There was a lot of that going around these days.

Eight

She was everything he wasn't, Joe told himself, standing out on the front porch, listening to the frogs and the cicadas, sipping on iced tea and wishing it were beer. She was soft and sweet. He was hard and bitter. She had a reason to look forward to the future. The only person he cared deeply about was eighty-three years old, and unless she pulled out of her depression pretty damned fast, she might not make eighty-four. Once she was gone....

Joe didn't want to think about when his grandmother was gone. He knew, though, that he would have to sell the house. That was a part of her will. Sell the house, split the take, half going to her favorite charity, half to be divided among her three heirs.

As far as Joe was concerned, they could have it all.

Miss Emma was home. The house was no more than a relic of the past.

At any rate, it was time to wind things up here and get on back. Tonight he'd have to lay it on the line, and tomorrow—what was that cliché? Go now, and don't look back?

Yeah. That, too.

Sophie was not quite as angry as she'd ever been in her life, but she was teetering on the brink. Not that she was frightened. At least, not any more. It was all over now, and nobody but poor Darryl had been hurt. All the same, she felt as if she'd been personally involved.

Thank goodness Joe had been here. Odd that she'd never once thought that he might have a hand in it. Was there something significant in that?

Probably. She wasn't going to think about it, though. Couldn't afford to.

With Iris settled, the two, new goldfish installed in the new aquarium and Joe waiting for her on the front porch, she couldn't think of another single reason for stalling, other than the fact that once she handed over the rest of the jade, he would leave. And it wasn't the jade she would miss, or the financial security it represented, as much as it was Joe himself. That was the saddest thought of all. You'd think that after a while a woman would learn.

As quiet as she was, she knew he heard the screen door. He didn't turn around. Just went on leaning against the white-painted post, a shadowy figure looking out at the lightning bugs and the occasional flicker of a car passing by out on the highway. He was holding something in his hand—a glass. Light from the living-room window gleamed on that and the band of his stainless-steel wristwatch, and highlighted the worn seat of his jeans.

Standing there in the doorway, Sophie stifled an irreverent urge to cup her palm under his taut buttocks and squeeze. If that didn't prove that she had buttermilk for brains, nothing could. A brand-new mother. A brand-new mother threatened with bankruptcy, whose house had just been burgled.

And she was lusting after the rear end of an ex-cop from Texas?

Oh, for mercy's sake!

"You coming out or staying in?" Joe asked.

"Out, I guess. No point in letting all the air-conditioning escape."

"It's noisy out here in the country, even though it's still so quiet."

"You miss all the big-city noises?"

"Not particularly. I dunno—yeah, maybe a few of 'em."

"I suppose if a person's inclined to be lonesome—"

"I'm not," he said quickly. She swallowed the barely realized hope that he would say he was and ask her what she could do about it.

Standing at the edge of the porch beside him, so close she could hear the slow, steady sound of his breathing, she said, "I'm not, either. I have too many plans now to even think about being lonely. I thought I'd wait until Iris is three months old and then start looking around for a job at a place that provides day care. Some of them do now. The bank says they'll give me a reference, and I can still write ad copy at night once I can afford to replace my computer, and—''

''Where is it, Sophie?''

''My computer? It was—''

''You know what I'm talking about. I don't think they got what they were looking for. I think that's the reason they did a job on the place. Because they couldn't find the jade, and they were mad as hell.''

She crossed her arms over her breasts. Scowling at the shadowy garden fence, she said, ''That's hardly my fault, is it? And anyway, how do you know it was a they, and not a him?''

''Or a her?'' So he told her about the tire tracks the deputy had found, that didn't match her car or his truck, and about the two sets of footprints, one male, one female. He'd missed those because he hadn't taken the time to search a big-enough perimeter, and because he'd been so damned concerned about Sophie.

What they said about doctors not treating their families went for cops, too. ''Quit stalling, honey. You're going to have to level with me, and we both know it. For Iris's sake, if not your own. They'll try again once I'm gone. This time your car and my truck were both gone. They knew the place was empty.''

''I don't want to hear this; I really don't.''

He persisted. "Maybe next time, they won't care who's home. What happens then?"

"There might not be a next time. You can't be sure they didn't find what they were looking for. Anyway, maybe they found out there's nothing here worth stealing."

"Where is it, Sophie?"

"Oh, for heaven's sake!" Sophie, whose nerves were frayed right down to the bone, flung out her hands, accidentally knocking the glass of iced tea from his grasp. Ice cubes flew out into her petunia bed. The glass hit the porch floor and rolled slowly off the edge. It was the last straw. She swore—something she didn't do often or well—and then burst into tears. Something she'd done entirely too much of lately.

Joe swore, too. As if it was the most natural thing in the world, he took her in his arms. Something hard inside him wanted to push his advantage. Something soft—he could've sworn there was nothing soft left—said, "Hey, now...it's not worth crying over. Nobody got hurt. If you'd had a decent burglar alarm, none of this would've happened." It was a lie, and they both knew it.

"Who'd hear the thing and call it in, my friendly neighbor down the road? All burglars know how to cut wires and things."

Joe wasn't about to go into the technicalities of a good security system. She couldn't afford much. Probably couldn't even afford to feed the dog he was going to give her, but that wasn't going to keep him from trying, on both counts.

She felt good in his arms. He tried to think brotherly, fatherly, avuncular thoughts, but it wasn't working. She was all woman. Warm, strong, smelling of baby powder and herbal soap. Any man who would take advantage of a woman at a time like this was three degrees lower than pond scum.

Not that he would. Not that he had any intention of doing anything more than seeing to her safety, recovering what he'd come for and heading west.

Sophie took a deep, steadying breath and slid her hands off his shoulders to push against his chest. He let her go instantly. She told herself it was a measure of her intelligence that she didn't throw herself at him again, because, truly, she would far rather hide in his arms for the next few years than do what had to be done.

"I'll go get the shovel." She sighed.

Joe tilted his head. "Come again?"

"Turn on the yard light, will you? It's the second switch inside the back door. Oh, and listen out for Iris while you're in there." She stepped off the porch and headed around the side of the house.

Curiouser and curiouser. Joe turned, went inside and then joined her a few minutes later in the backyard, at the far end of her vegetable garden.

He watched in silence as she planted her foot on the spade, pushed down cautiously and carefully lifted a few ounces of red Davie County clay. Watched as she did it again and again, and then he began to swear.

"Here's the first one," she said, handing him a

muddy plastic bag with something hard and lumpy inside.

She moved on to the next row and carefully repeated the exercise. Joe collected the bags. All twelve of them. One piece had been sold. Another, the Ch'ien Lung vase, was back in the Darryls' aquarium. He'd figured it was as safe a place as any.

But not as safe as under the first plant in each row of vegetables. "What ever made you bury it?"

"I don't have a safe. It was too bulky to fit into a deposit box, and besides, there's nothing wrong with burying valuables. People do it all the time."

"Sure they do." There'd been a joke going around headquarters a few years back about the con's wife who wrote to her husband in prison to tell him she'd buried the loot in the backyard.

A week later, she wrote again and told him the backyard was all dug up and ready for planting.

Sophie propped the shovel against the fence, dusted off her hands and turned toward the house. Joe, loaded down with muddy, lumpy plastic bags, followed.

It was all there. God knows what it was worth, Joe marveled. He wouldn't have given five bucks for the lot. Still, some of the carving was incredibly intricate. The color was nice enough, too, if you happened to like green: The stuff ranged from shades of faded khaki to iceberg lettuce. But of all the artifacts his grandfather had collected that were now scattered around his grandmother's sixteen-room, turn-of-the-century mansion, the jade was his least favorite. His own taste ran more to Navaho rugs and baseball memorabilia.

"So," she said. They were seated once again at the kitchen table, the jade spread out between them.

"So," he echoed, legs sprawled out, elbows on the table, the beginnings of a headache tugging at his hairline.

"I suppose it's just as well. To tell the truth, my conscience was starting to bother me. Once I found out what kind of a man Rafe was, I did wonder. Still, he said he collected antiques. He could've come by it honestly. And he did give it to me, but looking back, I don't think he'd really planned to. I just happened to walk in at the wrong time, and he said the first thing that popped into his mind." She sighed. Propping her chin in her hand, she nudged one of the muddy bags with her forefinger.

So Joe told her about the reward.

"Ten-thousand dollars," he heard himself saying. He'd originally thought five, but five grand didn't go very far these days. Ten might give her a better purchase on the future.

He could see it coming. All the telltale signs. Her eyes took on that glittery look. Her chin wobbled, lifted a notch or two and then firmed up again. The tip of her nose turned red.

"No," she said. "No, thank you."

He frowned. He hadn't bothered to read his bank statements lately, but he was pretty sure his trust fund could take the hit without even flinching. "Or maybe it was twenty, I forget."

"Joe, thank you. I know what you're trying to do, and I can't accept. But thank you."

It cost her to say it. He could tell by the way her voice rambled all over the scale. "I'm not trying to do anything. I'm only telling you that there's a reward for the recovery of the J. J. Dana collection. The stuff was insured, after all."

Sophie couldn't look at him. It was over. She'd known all along it would be this way. Now that he had what he'd come for, he would take it and leave. There wasn't a single reason why he should stay, and she would miss him. It was already starting to hurt. But she'd hurt before and healed, and she would heal this time, too.

Maybe next time she'd have the good sense not to let herself get emotionally involved with anyone who offered her a kind word. Even stray cats had better judgment.

"Sophie?"

"I've got some boxes out in the—oh, and you'll need tissue for wrapping each piece. There's a box of Christmas stuff in the—"

"Sophie, listen. About the reward. You might as well—"

"No. I told you, Joe, I'm not taking any reward for something that belongs to your grandmother. Let's just call it even, shall we? You helped me out when I needed a hand, and I'm glad I was able to return the favor."

He raked back his chair, stood and began to pace. Her kitchen wasn't all that big. She could feel the energy radiating off his lean, rangy body like heat waves rising off hot asphalt on a blistering summer day. "Well, for heaven's sake, I'd think you'd be happy! You came looking for your grandmama's jade whatnots and you found them, and it didn't cost you a blessed penny! What more do you want? Green stamps?"

His eyebrows went crooked. "Green stamps? What the dickens do you know about green stamps? They went out with Ozzie and Harriet."

"It's just something my mother used to say. At least, I think she did."

"Yeah, well, my mother used to say, 'But it was on sale, George. Look how much money I just saved you.' So now that we've swapped life histories, can we get back to the subject? If you won't take the money for yourself, take it for Iris. Kids are expensive to raise."

"I don't need charity."

Joe brushed both hands through his hair. He started counting. Out loud. He got as far as seven before he broke off. "Fine! Would you just tell me why not? At least tell me that!"

"Because I sold one of the pieces! It's gone. I can't pay you back because I don't have the money. If what it said on the back of the photograph is right, it was worth a lot more than I got for it, only I didn't know that at the time. The man at the antique shop offered me a hundred dollars at first—"

"A hundred dollars!" Joe's sun-bronzed face turned red. "You didn't—"

"No, of course not. Give me credit for better sense than that. He ended up paying—well, a lot more than that, at least."

He took a tight turn around the table and came to a halt with the toes of his worn Western boots about two inches from her muddy white sneakers. "Don't say anything. I don't want to know anymore. We'll just deduct whatever you got for it from the reward money, and your conscience will be in the clear."

"I said no, and I meant it. I don't want to fight with you about this, Joe. You got what you came for, so why can't you be happy?"

The sound he made came from somewhere deep in his throat. Taking her face between his hands, he forced her to meet his gaze, and because she couldn't help herself, she stared back. Defiantly, at first.

Neither of them spoke, but Sophie's breathing quickened. So did Joe's. He had touched her before, but never like this. She sensed anger, impatience, frustration and...something else. "Joe," she whispered.

"Don't say it." His breath was warm, sweet, soft. His hands were hard, callused, urgent. She couldn't have spoken if her life depended on it.

He was going to kiss her. Her lips softened, parted, and her eyelids drifted down. She felt her skirt brush against his legs as she moved imperceptibly closer. She took a deep breath...

And then felt the brush of his lips. Her knees threatened to buckle. She began to tremble. Moist, incredibly soft, he stroked her lips with his own as if afraid to commit to something deeper.

A familiar sound broke through her consciousness, and she thought, no, no—not now!

"Sophie," Joe murmured against her mouth.

"I know," she said the same way.

"I don't want to let you go."

But you will, she thought. *There was never any chance that you wouldn't.*

Pulling away was like trying to swim through cold molasses, but she did it. By the time she had arranged herself in the rocking chair, unbuttoned her blouse and settled her daughter to nurse, she'd stopped even hoping he would follow her.

Of course he wouldn't follow her. Why should he? There was nothing the least bit enticing about a flabby, badly dressed woman nursing a baby.

All the same, she sighed. Sighed and started thinking of all the adjustments she was going to have to make in her plans for the future. No waiting until Iris was three months old, for one thing. She'd have to send out résumés right away and see if she could borrow a PC from the agency so she could go on writing. It didn't bring in anywhere near enough to live on, but for the moment, it was all she had.

As for buying the house, option or no option, she might as well forget it. She'd be lucky to pay the rent.

Clothes. She'd have to start exercising right away so that once she found a job she could fit into her prepregnancy clothes, because she certainly couldn't afford to buy a new wardrobe. Her feet had grown half a size during her pregnancy, too. Somehow, she didn't think exercise was going to change that.

By the time she finished the nursing, burping and changing routine, she had things all pretty much settled in her mind. She had a strong tendency toward orderly thought...until just lately, that was.

Joe was nowhere to be found, which was probably just as well. She could hear his footsteps overhead. The bathroom mirror was steamy. Evidently he'd showered and gone up to bed.

With a sense of loss she didn't care to explore, she took her own shower, examined herself closely in the mirror for stretch marks and other indications of bodily changes, and went to bed.

Lord, she was tired! But then, considering all that had happened in the past twenty-four hours, it was no wonder.

In the middle of a dream, with no notion of what had disturbed her, Sophie came wide-awake. Sitting up in bed, she glanced over at the crib, which she'd moved into her bedroom. By the faint pink gleam of the night-light she could see the reassuring hump of Iris's bulky diapered bottom lifting the sheet.

She heard a thump. The sound came from the back of the house, not the front. Someone was in the kitchen.

Dear Lord, not again! Had Joe forgot to lock the pantry window?

Her first impulse was to call him, but she didn't. She was having a hard enough time as it was, convincing him that she was perfectly capable of looking after herself. She felt for her housecoat, didn't bother with slippers and walked silently to the door, avoiding the floorboard that always creaked.

There was a light coming from the kitchen. The door was shut, but it shone underneath. She could call 911 and wait for help, or she could throw open the door and scream for Joe. Knowing that any phone call she made could be heard easily from the kitchen, she chose the latter.

She had surprise on her side. Once she yelled, Joe would be down those stairs like a shot. Before the intruder could recover Joe would be on him, of that she hadn't the least doubt. It was what policemen did, after all. React to emergencies.

Her heart was thumping up against her esophagus. She forgot to breathe and then gulped air and had to stifle a cough. With her hand on the doorknob, she braced herself, flung open the door and screamed Joe's name.

Joe dropped the sugar bowl. Wearing nothing but boxers and boots, he stared at the apparition in the flapping flowered robe, her hair a wild nimbus around her flushed face.

"Huh?"

Shoulders slumping, she covered her face with both hands. "Oh, for heaven's sake," she whispered. Her eyes widened as peeping between her fingers, she took in what seemed to be vast stretches of naked flesh above and below his shorts.

He had a better build than she did. Smaller waist. Flatter abdomen. Shapelier legs, even if they were covered with short dark hair. He was lean, muscular and absolutely without doubt the most...

Swallowing hard, she forced her eyes above his chest. "I didn't mean to scare you."

"Did I wake you? I tried to be quiet, but I dropped the lid to the butter dish."

"I thought you were a burglar."

"Ah, jeez, honey, I'm sorry. I couldn't sleep, and I thought something to eat—" He held out the cheese, the butter and a jar of marmalade.

Sophie let out the breath she'd been holding. "It's all right. I had trouble, too. Getting to sleep, I mean. And then, when I did, I had a bad dream—all about being chased by a pirate with one of those great big curvy knives."

Joe set the food on the table. He'd already taken out the milk and bread. "Let me fix you a sandwich."

"My stomach's still quivering."

"Then milk's what you need. Lactating women—"

"I know about lactating women," she said repressively, pouring two glasses of two-percent and reaching for the reduced fat cheddar. "This hasn't been my day."

They ate in silent companionship. Sophie consciously avoided looking directly at his body, and after a while, the initial effect of all that raw masculinity began to wear off. She even went so far as to tell herself that if he so much as mentioned that damned jade, she was going to bop him with the marmalade jar.

But he didn't, and she didn't, and then Joe put the

remains into the refrigerator while Sophie rinsed out the glasses, and she thought, this is what having a husband would be like. Someone to share sleepless nights with. Someone to turn to when dreams go bad and things go wrong, and you need someone to hold you and not ask questions for which there aren't any answers.

"Ready to turn in?" he asked. She knew he was deliberately avoiding putting pressure on her. Pressure of any kind. And she appreciated it; she really did.

All the same, she wished he would hug her. A simple, friendly good-night hug. Was that too much to ask?

Evidently Joe picked up something in her attitude. Something about the hesitant way she reached for the light switch. The reluctant way she turned toward her own room.

"Still not sleepy?" he asked.

She shook her head. "But don't worry about it. As soon as I fall asleep, Iris will wake me up. Her timing is flawless."

"Then why don't I come in and keep you company until you wind down. We can sit over by the window and hold a whispered conference about colleges— about whether to send her to a military school or an all-girl's college. And about what kind of dog we're going to get—male or female."

"Oh, for—" she began when he took her by the hand, lifted a finger to his lips and said, "*Shhh*, don't wake the baby."

Nine

You got what you came for, man. Now get out. Get out before you get in any deeper!

But Joe knew he wasn't going to do it. He was courting disaster, but hell—he'd been doing that on a regular basis all his life. So what else was new?

There were two chairs in her bedroom, a straight chair and the wicker rocker from the nursery. He took the rocker. At least his survival instinct was keeping him out of her bed.

So far.

Iris didn't stir. Sophie looked as if she didn't know where to go, what to do or say. He couldn't much blame her. This was uncharted territory. He'd lain awake in the bed upstairs for hours after he'd turned in, reliving that kiss. Wanting to pick up where they'd left off, even knowing that under the circumstances, it couldn't go any farther than that.

He was no kid anymore. When he kissed a woman—really kissed her—it usually led to sex. The fact that he hadn't kissed a woman, or come anywhere near it, for a long time, might explain why he was in the condition he was in right now.

If he had any brains, he'd get up, pack his duffel and get the hell out of here, right now. He'd done what he'd set out to do. Mission accomplished. No way was he going to give her grief for selling a piece of the collection. Q.E.D., as his old algebra teacher used to say. It stood for something profound in Latin, like "That's a wrap, guys, I'm outta here."

He shifted his weight in the rump-sprung old wicker chair. It creaked. Iris made a sucking noise in her sleep. Sophie leaned back and lifted her feet up onto the bed, and in the dim pink glow of the night-light Joe thought she was starting to look drowsy.

He yawned and shifted again on the thin chintz-covered cushion. It occurred to him that he ought to apologize for showing up for the party in his under-wear, but then, why bother? She hadn't even noticed it. Not nearly as much as he'd noticed that old-flowered wrapper of hers. With the sash knotted at the waist, she looked ripe and soft and womanly. All the things he was drawn to for all the wrong reasons.

"I'd better go and let you get some sleep." He cov-ered a yawn. Funny thing—for a woman who turned him on the way she did, she was surprisingly restful.

Easygoing. That was another way of saying it. Joe

had never been around such a woman before. His sisters were so uptight he came away from a session with either of them wrung-out and ready for a drink. Before her stroke, Miss Emma had been a lavender-scented, lace-edged martinet. As for Leeza, his ex-wife, she was about as soothing as a cheap banjo strung too tight and played too fast.

"I'm afraid I'll dream again," Sophie murmured.

"Then make sure it's a good one."

"How do you do that?" she asked with a plaintive little smile that tugged at something buried deep inside him. "Is there a formula for good dreams?"

Several moments ticked by. And then she said, "Joe, I don't suppose you'd..."

"Don't suppose I'd what?"

"Oh, nothing. Go to bed, I'll be just fine."

"You don't suppose I'd do what, Sophie?"

"Honestly, it's not important. I was just thinking about something I used to do when I was a little girl, whenever I had a bad dream. I couldn't have been very old—I can't even remember it all that well—but I do recall running into Mama's bedroom this one time, tripping over her slippers and crying because I split my lip when I struck the edge of the bed."

Joe's eyes widened. His body came slowly to attention. "You want to trip over my slippers?"

She laughed. Softly, so as not to wake the baby. "Of course not, I meant Mama used to take me into her bed and hold me whenever I had a bad dream, and it felt so—oh, I don't know. I told you it was silly."

"So what, honey? It felt so what? So safe?" he

prompted, and she nodded, her eyes speaking the words she lacked the courage to voice.

Joe, grateful for the shadows that concealed his instant reaction, came slowly to his feet. If she had any idea what he was thinking right now, he told himself, safe was the very last thing she'd be feeling. Which made it all the more curious that a few minutes later he found himself lying in her bed. A bed that smelled of Sophie, sunshine and herbal soap. Lying there on his side, with one arm around her, her soft behind pressed up against his throbbing groin and her hair tickling his chin.

He started counting down backward from a hundred.

She made a little sound in her throat that reminded him of a purring cat. Desperately, he visualized ice bergs and counted those. He tried to pretend he was swimming upstream in a cold, white-water river.

When none of that worked, he groped for a topic of conversation.

"You've never mentioned your father. What was he like?"

"I don't know much about him, really. His name was Sam, and he was in the army in Vietnam. I seem to remember Mama saying he went to Alaska with a lady and two gentlemen friends—I used to picture him racing dogsleds across frozen deserts. I'm not sure, but I don't think Mama ever heard from him after he left us."

So he asked about her mother and she told him the basics, or as much as came to mind. "Her name was

Althea and she drank hot tea instead of coffee and kept dried flowers in paper bags in the closet. I was six— I'd just started the first grade—when she took me to this big brick building one day and told me she had to go away for a while, but she'd always be within call if I needed her.''

Ah, jeez, Joe thought, *I don't want to hear this.* He had too many memories of his own, dating from about that same age.

''I kept thinking she'd come back. I waited and waited, but she never did. Then one day I overheard one of the teachers talking to the housekeeper about poor Mrs. Bayard, who'd died of some awful disease called metastasis. It wasn't until years later that I learned she'd had breast cancer.''

Joe could only embrace her. He couldn't take away the pain of her loss. As sad as her story was, he'd heard sadder. For fourteen years he'd been exposed to the seamiest side of darkness. That was the downside of being a cop.

He stroked her shoulder and fitted himself more closely around her body. ''My folks died when I was eleven. Did I mention I have a couple of younger sisters, Donna and Daisy? Any parent who'd name a child Donna Dana—well, you have to wonder.''

He'd hoped for a chuckle, but there was no response. Moments later he heard that puffy little sound she made with her lips when she was dozing.

Mission accomplished. Time to go.

He didn't stir.

Move it, sergeant!

Joe knew he'd walked into this one with his eyes wide open. She'd asked him to hold her the way her mother had held her. In another woman he might have suspected an ulterior motive—a ploy designed to further her own interests. But not Sophie. What interests could she possibly have that he could further?

Lust?

On his part, sure. Enough so that he was surprised she hadn't noticed back there in the kitchen.

But she'd just had a baby. It was too soon, even if she'd been interested. If it was about the jade, they both recognized he wasn't going to give it back. He couldn't. And she'd refused everything else he had offered.

With a quiet little sigh, she drew up one knee, shifting her hips in the process. Joe ground his teeth and told himself he could handle it. One of the things he'd better remind her of before he left, though, was that women didn't invite men into their beds without risking certain consequences.

One of those consequences was in that crib on the other side of the room. And that was one of the more benign consequences. Where the devil had she been all these years, hiding out in the cabbage patch?

He was about as far from sleep as he'd ever been, but brainpower wasn't going to pull him out of this one. Unfortunately, his intellect didn't function below the belt. The only sensible thing to do was to get up, pull on his clothes and get out.

Which he vowed to do, just as soon as he could make arrangements to get her house secured. He'd formed some pretty definite ideas along those lines. The first project in his new career as a security specialist, you might say.

She needed a dog. The right kind of dog would make a big difference. He'd see to that, and maybe a good fence, too. Chain link, not chicken wire. He ought to be able to talk her into accepting that much at least. For Iris's sake.

As for the leaky roof...

Oh, hell. Maybe he could arrange for her to win a lottery.

Sophie rocked and sang softly so as not to disturb Joe. She couldn't believe she'd actually invited the man into her bed, but there he was, sleeping peacefully between her flowered sheets. She'd woken up in his arms, her hair trapped under his shoulder, one of his legs draped over her thigh. She blamed it on the fact that she'd been startled out of a dream in the middle of the night. There was something about the hours between two and four o'clock in the morning that lent themselves to all manner of fantasies. The illogical magically became logical. The impossible, possible.

Even now, with the sunlight streaming in through her window, slanting across a muscular masculine chest and a lot of crisp, dark body hair, it still seemed right.

He stirred. She shifted Iris to her other breast, suddenly aware of a sense of well-being that was frightening in its very intensity. Knowing perfectly well that it was only an illusion, she set out to enjoy it while she could. Perfect moments were never lasting ones. Daydreams, rainbows, morning glories and dew-spangled spiderwebs—all were ephemeral, but none the less precious for it.

She sighed, feeling a familiar warmth against her forearm. "You're wet, sweetheart," she murmured, and Joe groaned and turned over.

"Hmm?"

"Not you," she said, smiling. Wanting to laugh. Wanting to crawl into bed with her baby and hold them both close for a little longer.

The phone rang. Joe opened his eyes. "Who on earth—" she wondered aloud as she shifted Iris onto her shoulder.

"I'll get it." He was up, his eyes alert, before she could even finish running down the list of people who might be calling her before eight o'clock in the morning.

He reached the phone first. She was right behind him. "It's my phone, after all," she muttered. There were times when the man was impossibly bossy. She didn't know if it was a policeman thing, a Texas thing or a male thing.

"Joe?" she whispered. He'd identified himself and was paying attention to someone on the other end. "Joe, who in the world is it?" she persisted.

He held up a hand for silence, then listened another few seconds. "Right. Keep me posted, will you?"

The instant he hung up, she said, "Well, for heaven's sake, are you going to tell me, or not?"

"Sheriff's office. They caught two people in Randolph County—where the hell is Randolph County, anyway?''

Sophie waved a hand in a generally southeasterly direction. ''Caught who? Are they our burglars?''

''Possibly.'' He raked a hand across his stubbled jaw and grimaced. It occurred to Sophie that he ought to look like the very devil, with his beard, his rumpled shorts, his rumpled hair and his bony, bare feet.

Instead he looked beautiful. Like a sexy, grumpy bear fresh out of hibernation. When he scratched his chest, furthering the image, she had to smile. ''Well, I'm glad that's over. Now we don't have to worry anymore. Who are they?''

''I said possibly. It's too soon to know. Look, if you don't want the bathroom right now, I need a liberal dose of cold water applied externally.''

''Jo-oe,'' she wailed plaintively, watching him disappear into her one bathroom.

By the time he joined her in the kitchen, Iris had been changed and put down for a nap. Sophie had brushed her hair, tied it back and slathered moisturizer on her face. The window unit was struggling to get ahead of the August heat and humidity, and she was trying hard not to dwell on what she would do after he left. Which would probably be later on today.

She couldn't think of a single reason why he shouldn't leave today, except that she was dangerously close to doing the unthinkable. Falling in love. Again.

''So who did it?'' she asked.

Instead of answering her, he said, ''I'll cook if you want to grab a shower.''

"Cooking's woman's work."

"Female chauvinist. The world's best chefs are all men."

"Not anymore they're not, but thanks, I guess I will. You're obviously not going to talk until you're good and ready." She handed over the spatula, shot him an exasperated look and left, imagining several wildly inappropriate thoughts, none of which concerned the pair of suspects being held in Randolph County.

Hormones, she chided herself as she stripped off her robe and gown and turned on a rusty trickle of lukewarm water. It had to be hormones. If jangled postpartum hormones could cause depression in certain women, they could just as easily cause this crazy, head-over-heels-in-love syndrome.

"Your antique dealer, so far as we know, isn't involved. A woman who worked for him apparently is. Whenever anything interesting came in for appraisal, she'd make a note of the particulars and then she and her boyfriend would go after it. They specialized in antique jewelry but weren't above heisting small furniture, art—anything that could be sold to another dealer."

"Oh, poor Mr. Lorris. I know he was crushed when he found out. He tried to chisel me, but he was nice about it when I refused his first few offers. I sort of thought he respected me until I found out how much more the thing was worth than what he ended up paying me for it."

Joe shrugged. He'd put on a shirt. The collar was damp where his wet hair had dripped on it. There was a nick on his jaw where he'd cut it shaving. Sophie gathered up all these little imperfections and stored them away to use against the heartache that was heading her way.

"He'll be questioned. You might be called on to testify, but that shouldn't be a problem."

It shouldn't, but she wasn't looking forward to it. "I guess you'll be leaving now. I don't know how to—"

"Don't." Joe stirred the third spoonful of sugar into his coffee. "We aren't done yet, Sophie. I told you I was going to see about a security system, and—"

"And I said I'd do it myself."

"Yeah, sure you will. You can't even remember whether or not you shut the windows."

"You're not being fair. I've looked after myself for years, and nothing like this has ever happened to me before. And you'll have to admit, I've had cause for being distracted lately."

"Yeah, well, one little distraction is all it takes. And this isn't the first time you've been ripped off, remember? Or don't you count the father of your child?"

She caught her breath. "That's low."

"It was meant to be." He spared her nothing. Not the intensity of his dark eyes. Not the grim set of his razor-nicked jaw. "Now, I've checked out several firms around these parts and found a dealer for a system that's just right for your place. I'm meeting a guy here this morning, and we'll get started. Next we'll go pick out your dog, and then see about fencing in the place so he'll have room to run.''

Silently, Sophie began to name the twelve apostles. It was something she'd been taught to do as a child whenever her temper threatened to get out of hand. She got as far as Matthew, and then she gave Joe the benefit of her opinion.

''You want to know what you can do with your dog? I'll tell you what you can do with your dog, and your fence, and…and your security system!''

''Now, Sophie—''

''You can put them in your truck and take them back to Texas with you! I'll even pack your bag!'' She was so blessed furious she could cry.

Joe held out a placating hand. ''Now, simmer down, honey, I know what you're thinking.''

''Don't you honey me, you…you—! If you knew half of what I'm thinking, you'd be clean over the county line by now!''

''With my tail feathers smoking, right?''

''I'm not joking, Joe. I think you'd better leave right now. You've got a long drive ahead of you, and since you have what you came for there's nothing to keep you here. As for the piece I sold, I'm just as sorry as I can be, but I can't get it back. It's gone. Maybe your grandmama's insurance will cover it.''

He made an impatient sound and started to speak, but she cut him off. ''I'll always be grateful to you for all you've done, but enough is enough. I don't *want* your security system. I don't *want* a dog. I don't want *anything* that I can't afford to pay for myself, and no, I am *not* going to take any reward money!''

"Why? Just tell me that, Sophie—why do you have to be so damned stubborn? It's not like I was trying to bribe you or anything. All I want is to leave you with a little basic protection. All I want is to be able to go home without having a crazy woman and her baby on my conscience."

"You want me to take that one item at a time?" She was quietly seething. "In the first place, I am neither crazy nor stubborn. In the second place, your conscience is the least of my worries. If my daughter needs protection, I'll see to it myself. In the third place..."

What was the third place?

"Oh, yes. The reward. I refuse to take a reward I don't deserve, and—"

"That's crazy!"

"Hush up, it's my turn to talk! I'm not going to take it because once I found out what kind of a man Rafe was, I should have taken the stuff straight to the police and told them to find the owner. And I didn't. Instead I convinced myself it was a freewill gift, and I sold one piece and spent the money. Spent it wisely, I might add, but it wasn't mine to use. And then I buried the rest, fully intending to dig it up a piece at a time and spend it every bit as sensibly as I did the first. But I'll get along just fine without it, so no thank you for your reward. And now, if you don't mind, I'd like to...to be alone."

Joe looked at her as if she'd suddenly sprouted a second head.

Sophie almost wished she had. The first one certainly wasn't living up to its guarantee.

Ten

Joe liked the German shepherd. Sophie hated him on sight. The big dog was arrogant, and she'd had about all the male arrogance she cared to endure in one morning. She'd been *that close* to winning the argument when the man from Syncho Systems had driven up in his big blue van, slammed a door and called out a greeting.

And then Iris had tuned up. By the time she'd finished nursing and changing her, there were men tromping all over her house with Joe, swaggering around in his boots, his wide-shouldered shirt and his narrow-hipped jeans, taking charge as if he had every right. When she'd protested, he'd just grinned that lazy, sexy, maddening grin of his, and then one thing had led to another and now here she was, shopping for a dog.

She was a pushover. So what else was new?

"What's wrong with that one?" She pointed several cages down to an overweight, short-legged, charcoal gray mongrel with scraggly hair and an apologetic look.

"We're shopping for a guard dog, not a mudroom doormat."

"I like her. She reminds me of someone I used to know." She strolled over to where the animal stood, nose to the wire, gazing up hopefully with a pair of small, pink-rimmed eyes. She had a skin problem. She was as wide as she was long. "All you need is a decent chance, isn't that right, Lady?" Kneeling, Sophie poked a finger through the wire and allowed the dog to sniff.

"Honey, come away now. She'll think you're serious."

Every time he called her honey, even though it didn't mean anything, Sophie felt a quickening around her heart. "I am serious," she informed him.

Joe stared at her. Didn't have to speak, the look said it all.

"Well, if I have to have a dog, then I'm going to have the one I want," she said impatiently. "I don't feel a speck of...of rapport with any of those animals you've showed me so far. They all look vicious to me."

He'd showed her two German shepherds and a boxer-rottweiler mix. The rest of the four-legged residents were either too small, too old, too friendly or of the feline persuasion.

"Why don't we take another look at the—"

"No."

"Sophie, be reasonable. We're not talking house pets here, we're talking guard dogs. If you'd rather, we can still go to the breeder." They'd come to the animal shelter only because Sophie insisted that it was the humane thing to do. Far be it from Joe to hand her any more ammunition to use against him. He'd set out to prove he could be as humane as the next guy.

All he'd proved so far was that he could be as big a sucker.

Lady rode in the back of the truck with the camper shut, because Sophie was afraid she might become disoriented and try to jump out.

Joe figured she couldn't have made it over the tailgate if the truck caught fire, but he wasn't about to argue. He could fumigate the camper later, and hose it out.

Sophie hurried Iris into the house as soon as they pulled up out front. It was that time again. Joe didn't need to check a clock, or even to hear the baby fussing. All he had to do was look at Sophie's breasts. Something he'd been doing entirely too much of lately. How was it possible for a nursing mother to turn him on the way she did? Was she even aware of it? Why did she think he spent so much time sitting around with a newspaper spread over his lap?

It was getting to be embarrassing.

Retrieving a coil of clothesline from the back stoop, he glanced at the door and thought about going inside—in case she needed help or anything like that. "Woman, you've got me tied up in more knots than a Boy Scout troop," he grumbled.

He had to drag the mangy mutt out of his truck. She took one look at the coil of rope over his shoulder and dug in her toenails. "Come on, you sorry old fleabag, it's not a hangman's noose. I'm just going to hitch you to the trellis while I build you a temporary pen."

Sophie called the mutt Lady. Joe thought of her as Tramp. Using a roll of rusty chicken wire and some half-rotted fence posts he found leaning up against the ramshackle shed in the backyard, he set to work. While he had every intention of having a chain-link security fence installed before he left, it could take a few days. A couple of days to convince Sophie—another day or so to get it built.

Meanwhile, Tramp needed a pen of some sort, or else he'd have to shut her up in the shed or keep her tied to the trellis. No point in even having a guard dog unless it was free to patrol the perimeter.

Guard dog. That was a laugh!

Fortunately he'd soon have a first-class security system in place, including new locks and stoppers on all the windows. No system was foolproof, but this one should do the job for her. He could go back home with a clear conscience.

When Sophie came out to announce lunch and examine his handiwork, the job was nowhere near finished. Joe had managed to break the shovel handle, bruise two fingers and a foot. He'd also acquired a lump on his forehead when a fence post had fallen over and caught him off guard, and that was only for starters. The mutt had chewed her rope in two, then promptly sprawled out in the sun beside the ragged ends and gone to sleep. Which proved she was either smarter than she looked or totally brain-dead, he wasn't sure which.

"Handy with tools, are we?" Sophie drawled. He shot her a resentful look, placed a hand on the small of his back and straightened up. She was teasing him. He figured it was a good sign. At least if she could joke about it, it meant she was resigned to being protected.

"I can change a tire and program a VCR," he said modestly. Mopping the sweat from his brow with a mud-streaked forearm, he winced when he came in contact with his rapidly darkening lump.

"Me, too. More to the point, I can make iced tea and bacon, lettuce, cheese and tomato sandwiches. Could I interest you in any of the above?"

She could have interested him in a good dousing with a garden hose at the moment. "Sounds good. I'd better clean up some first, though."

He limped after her as far as the back door, admiring the subtle sway of her hips, telling himself she was doing it deliberately—knowing she wasn't.

Pausing on the back stoop, he began easing a muddy boot off one foot while he hopped around on the other, which didn't do his bum knee any good. It was a painful process. Evidently he'd bruised a bone or two in his foot when he'd missed the hole with the shovel and come down in the wrong place with the business end. The handle had gotten busted when he'd tried to wrap the damned thing around a sapling.

"Did you hurt your foot?"

He glared at her. She was standing in the back doorway, looking calm, cool and clean in a sleeveless, sunflower-printed dress. "No, I didn't hurt my foot," he snarled.

"Hot Epsom salts might help."

"It's nothing, not worth worrying over."

"What if it swells up and you can't get your boots on again?"

"Look, I just struck it a glancing blow with the damned shovel, all right?"

"You're hungry, aren't you?"

"Yeah...I reckon."

Joe was thoroughly ashamed of himself. From the time he'd gone to live with his grandparents he'd been taught the proper way to treat a lady. Hell, he'd even had to be polite to his sisters!

But he'd overslept this morning, thanks to lying awake, wondering what she'd say if he were to climb in bed with her again. After a sleepless night, before he'd even had time to grab a bite of breakfast, the crew had come to get started on the security system. Sophie had climbed back up on her high horse, so he'd invented an appointment with a dog breeder and hustled her and the baby out of there before she could cause trouble.

And then ended up taking her from one county

pound to another until she'd found what she was looking for.

He was finally learning how to handle her. The trick was to be firm and devious at the same time. Arguing against her brand of logic didn't work.

"You broke the shovel on your foot?" she asked now, all innocence. "Oh, my—that must have hurt!"

Joe shot her a sour look. He'd scored close to the top on every test he'd taken in all his years on the force. Blindfolded, he could dismantle his service revolver, clean it, put it back together and reload faster than any other man in the department. He'd even worked with the bomb squad for a couple of years.

But when it came to anything involving hammer, nails and a handsaw, he was strictly out of his element, a failing he put down to having spent his formative years around a slew of servants who did everything but cut his meat for him.

He limped inside in his sock feet and washed up at the sink. Miss Emma would've had a fit.

Which might've been good for her, come to think of it.

Joe was on his second messy, delicious sandwich when he remembered the dog. "Oh, hell, I forgot to tie the tramp up again," he said, raking back his chair and limping toward the front door.

Sophie was right behind him. "Lady won't run away." He gave her that look again. "Well, she won't. She knows where her home is, don't you, darling?"

The dog was on the porch, right outside the screen door. Her stub of a tail gyrating, she was grinning like a hyena. "I think she's still hungry," Sophie said in that tone of voice women reserved for babies and small fuzzy animals. "Maybe I'd better fix her another plate."

"She's already had a pork chop, applesauce and potato salad. What she needs is to lose a few pounds. Not to mention a few thousand fleas."

"It's not her fault she's been neglected. I'm going to shampoo her as soon as I put the dishes in to soak."

Joe grumbled something under his breath about hedge clippers and kerosene and stalked off, wondering, not for the first time, why he was still here. Why he hadn't left as soon as he'd gotten what he'd come for. It wasn't as if he didn't have family, friends and some unfinished business waiting for him back in Dallas.

So how come instead of getting on with his life, he kept finding one excuse after another to hang around in a seedy old house with a nutty female and her fat-faced daughter, doing the kind of work that could cripple a man if he weren't careful?

It was almost dark when Sophie stepped outside to inspect the pen Joe had finally managed to put together. To the west, past the grove that surrounded a nearby creek, streaks of slate gray cloud fingered their way across a hazy gold sunset. She paused long enough to admire the effect and to enjoy listening to the familiar sounds of crickets and tree frogs, chimney swifts and distant traffic.

Home. She'd been here less than six months, but

already it felt more like home than her apartment in town ever had. Evidently she was a nest-builder by nature.

"Well, what do you think?" Joe called to her, and she went on down the steps and out into the backyard.

Joe had wanted to call a fencing company and have some fancy, highfalutin security fence put in, but she'd drawn the line at that. Told him she didn't need it and couldn't afford it. Back in the spring when she'd first moved out to the country, she'd explored the shed and discovered—besides a few basic gardening tools, some canning jars and a five-foot rat snake—several rolls of rusty chicken wire. She'd used a roll and a half around her garden.

Joe, it seemed, had used the rest. Trying hard not to laugh, she examined the oddly shaped, haphazardly fastened wire pen. He'd used three posts—all of them leaning at a different angle—two trees, and a corner of the shed. She didn't know where he'd found all the nails, but the supports were practically bristling with them, all driven halfway in and bent over.

A carpenter he was not.

"Hmm," she said thoughtfully. "She'll need a place to sleep."

"I already thought of that. There's a fifty-five gallon drum out behind your shed. I'll roll it into the pen, tip it onto its side and rake up some pine straw to make a bed."

Sophie had in mind a folded blanket in one corner of the kitchen, but that could wait until after Joe left. Which would be most any day now. Maybe when the time came, having a dog in the house would help to distract her. Keep her from dwelling on things best forgotten. Such as how much she was going to miss his bossiness. His steadiness. His unfailing kindness. His humor. The way he looked holding Iris. Those sweet, sexy, smiles that made her imagine all sorts of impossible, inappropriate thoughts.

By the time they'd finished supper and Sophie had settled Iris for the next few hours, Joe was moving as if every bone in his body ached. Coming in through the back door after checking on the dog, he collapsed onto a kitchen chair. The knot on his head had gone down, but he was obviously hurting more than he would admit.

"I told you to soak your foot," she said.

"I thought you said to soak my head."

She would've expected him to complain. Instead he teased. There was a lot to like about Joe Dana. She ran him a basin of hot water, knelt beside his chair and set it carefully on the floor. "A bathtub full would be better, but by the time the tub fills up, the water's already cooled off. Number one on my list of things to be done as soon as I sell—" Guiltily she lifted her eyes to his. "Oops."

"There's always the reward. That ought to cover a complete plumbing overhaul, a new roof and a set of new tires."

Sophie thought it best to change the subject. Dipping her elbow into the water, she said, "There, that feels just about right." She dumped in half a box of

Epsom salts and ordered, "Now, roll up your pant leg."

He leaned over and groaned, and she brushed his hands away and said, "Oh, for heaven's sake," and did the job herself. "For someone supposedly in the prime of life—a man who looks as if he's spent years riding the range under a hot, Texas sun—you're in terrible shape."

And then she listened while he told her that contrary to popular belief, not every man from Texas wore chaps and a ten-gallon hat and spent his life *ya— hooing* back and forth across the prairie.

"Then why do you wear cowboy boots?"

"They're not cowboy boots."

"They have pointy toes and high heels."

"They do not have high heels!"

"Why not wear sneakers, or cross trainers, or something like that? Most men do when they're out in the country."

"Dammit, I'm not most men!"

Sophie, still on her knees after rolling up the leg of his jeans, looked up. Once again their eyes caught and held. "No, you're not," she said quietly, deciding he could read into that what he will.

It was the truth. The longer he stayed, the more she realized that Joe Dana was like no other man she'd ever known. If she'd been asked to write down a list of specifications for the perfect man, Joe wouldn't have come within a mile of qualifying.

He wasn't Hollywood handsome.

He was impatient to the point of surliness.

He dressed like a—well, he was on the road, after all, she rationalized. He probably hadn't packed much besides jeans and khaki shirts. All the same, she couldn't imagine him in a suit and tie, much less a policeman's uniform. Eddie Dinsmore looked as if he'd been born in a suit and tie. She couldn't imagine him in anything else.

And Eddie Dinsmore was about as exciting as wet bread.

Sophie sighed.

Joe reached out and laid a hand on her head. Just that. He didn't say a word, but all the same, she read in that one simple gesture all the things she wanted to hear.

I'm sorry to be such a bear. Sorry I insulted your dog. Sorry I offended your pride. Sorry I'm not the man you want me to be.

Sorry he couldn't hang around long enough to woo her and win her and marry her and live happily ever after?

She sighed again and got to her feet, feeling exhausted, discouraged, overly emotional. Once more, she blamed it on her hormones. How long did it take to get back to normal after having a baby?

However long it took, Joe would be gone.

It rained again in the night. Sophie got up to close windows. To save on her power bill, she usually turned off the air conditioners once the heat of the day was gone, preferring to open the house and let the cool evening air flow through.

She awoke with a headache. Sinuses, she told herself.

Joe was in the kitchen, fumbling around on the shelf where she kept her various pills. "Headache," he muttered.

"That lump on your forehead."

Funny, she thought. With any other man she'd be embarrassed at being seen with her hair all tangled and her rumpled cotton nightgown with the milk stains on the front.

This time he'd put a shirt on over his white boxers. It didn't help. All she could think was that he was here now, and soon he would be gone. There were so many things they hadn't done together that she wanted to do. So many things they hadn't talked about. Against all reason, she had come to think of him as belonging to her, yet for all she knew, there might be a special woman waiting back in Dallas.

Unless all the single women in Texas were out of their minds, there had to be.

"Tramp's sacked out in her barrel. I shone a flashlight out there, and she didn't even stir. Great watchdog you've got there."

"I had a dog named Lady when I was little. She looked a lot like this Lady, only smaller. I used to sneak her into my room after Mama went to sleep, thinking I was getting away with something, only looking back, I'm pretty sure Mama knew. The bed always smelled doggy, and there were probably dog hairs, too. I never even thought to brush the sheets before I pulled up the spread."

Chatter, chatter, chatter. As if he were interested. Embarrassed, she watched as he poured out four tablets, handed Sophie two, popped two into his mouth, and then drank from the faucet. Sophie got herself a glass. "You can't swallow pills with your head upside down," she chided.

"Sure you can. What happened to her?" Joe asked, wiping his mouth on his sleeve. She couldn't imagine another man doing that without looking like a real slob. On Joe, it looked sexy.

On Joe, everything looked sexy. That was the trouble.

"When I moved to the Dunwiddy Home for Children of Veterans of Foreign Wars, I had to leave her behind. They didn't allow dogs. I made myself believe she got adopted, but she was probably taken to the pound."

"That explains today," he said as the noise of the rain increased.

Wordlessly she nodded. It wasn't dogs on her mind now. Nor headaches, nor even rain-spattered windowsills.

"I've always loved hearing rain on the roof after I've gone to bed." The small revelation was accompanied by a determined lift of her chin. "I'll probably sleep like a log now."

Leaning his hips against the counter, Joe met her gaze, his eyes saying things she wanted to believe and couldn't afford to.

"Yes, well...I'd better..."

"Sophie, do you really want me to go back upstairs?"

She lifted her shoulders and let them fall. Her fingers slid slowly back and forth on the hard, smooth surface of the tumbler.

"I want to hold you." His voice was low and raspy, but his meaning was unmistakable. "I want to do a lot more than hold you, but we both know that can't happen."

Eleven

It can't happen, her mind echoed. And yet, Sophie thought, something was happening. Something momentous was happening as they stood there barefoot in her kitchen, cool, damp air flowing in through the window, stirring her gown against her naked skin—pressing his open shirt against his side.

If he had touched her with his hands instead of his gaze, she couldn't have felt it more intensely. She forgot to breathe. He didn't. She could see the flutter of a pulse against his damp, bronzed throat—hear the rasp of his quickened breathing.

"I'd like that," she whispered. "For you to hold me—just for tonight."

"Just for tonight," he repeated, something that sounded almost like regret coloring the words.

With his arm at her waist, he led her down the hall to her bedroom. Sophie was glad she'd moved Iris back to the nursery. Just like a husband and wife, she thought. As if we'd been lovers forever. In a way, it seemed almost as if they had.

In another way, she was more than ever aware of a feeling of enormous loss. Of a magic that had come so close—so close she could feel the warmth of it, see the glow—and then gone away, leaving her in the darkness.

Just as they had before, he held open the covers and she slipped between the sheets. There was no question of undressing, but she couldn't help but think, what if we did? What then?

It was too soon.

And far, far too late...

Just as they had the last time, Sophie lay on her right side and Joe moved in behind her, fitting his body around hers. His arm came around her, his left hand closing over her wrist. She always slept on her side with one fist curled under her chin.

Her hand covered his. She could feel his breath stirring in her hair. Breathing in the scent of his body, she recognized her own bayberry soap and something that was essentially male—essentially Joe. Something musky, spicy, unmistakably sexual in nature.

Sophie was not widely experienced. There had been two men in her life—Rafe and the man she'd briefly been engaged to marry. Yet it was as if she'd never before lain with a man. As if Joe were a different species.

"Are you asleep?" he whispered.

"No, are you?" He wasn't. She could tell. She could feel his arousal stirring against her hips. Feel the quickening of his breath and the heavy beat of his heart against her back.

Instead of answering, he moved his hand until it closed over her breast. She uttered a sound like a soft, openmouthed groan, and he said, "Did I hurt you?"

Beyond speech, she shook her head. His hand cupped her, his thumb stroked her, and she wondered wildly if it was only her rampaging hormones again—if she would've responded to any man who had touched her this way....

She thought about how a man's body could react to a woman's body without even knowing who she was, whereas a woman did so with her heart long before she reacted with her body. But then that wasn't entirely true, either. Neither her heart nor her body had ever responded so enthusiastically to any man. Every instinct she possessed told her they were meant to be together.

Yes, and every shred of intellect told her it wasn't going to happen. She had no business even thinking of such a thing at a time like this—yet she had never felt more sexually alive. According to the experts, brand-new mothers weren't supposed to be interested in sex. Husbands traditionally complained because all wives thought about was their babies. Did that mean she was an unnatural mother? Oversexed? Desperate?

Or did it just mean that Joe was here now, and she'd

learned to make the most of today because her to-
morrows had never been certain?

She gasped his name as his fingers plucked ever so
gently at her nipple. He stroked the sensitive tip with
the open palm of his hand, sending currents of elec-
tricity to the very tips of her toes.

His lips were nuzzling the side of her neck. When
he said, "Mmm," without ever lifting them, she felt
that, too, and shivered as the heat of his hand burned
through her thin cotton nightgown. He was hot, hard,
aggressively aroused, and yet his touch was so gentle
she felt like taking his hand in hers and moving it to
where she ached the most.

As if he could read her mind—read her body's
needs—he slid his hand slowly down over her waist
and spread his fingers over her soft, newly flat
belly—and then lower still.

"You make me crazy," he whispered.

"I'm not supposed to be feeling this way," she said
helplessly.

"How do you feel, Sophie? What do you want?"

She gave a sob of laughter. "You must know. As
for what I want…" Her voice tapered off as his hands
began to work their magic.

"Yeah—me, too. Crazy, isn't it? None of this was
supposed to happen."

She could feel him moving rhythmically against her,
instinctively seeking the same release she so desperately needed. And it wasn't going to happen.

Unless…

"Joe, do you think we could—"

And then his hand began to move, too, his fingers tenderly exploring her, and she stiffened and then sighed and pressed herself into his touch. By the time he focused his attention on that one tiny pleasure point, she was so far beyond reason that it didn't matter anymore that none of this should be happening. In a way she couldn't put into words—wouldn't dare, even if she could—it was right.

All too soon she shattered under his tender assault.

Shattered, cried out, and shed a few tears because it was over. And as wonderful as it was—for her, at least—she wanted more. Wanted him inside her, a part of her.

"Sophie, Sophie," he whispered, holding her tightly, stroking her back. Her gown was rucked up around her waist, and he lifted her and slipped it off over her head. "Let me hold you this way, darling, just for a little while, will you?"

He was all but naked. She could feel him, smooth and hard and throbbing against her thighs, and with a small inarticulate cry, she reached down and took him in her hands.

"You don't have to—" he protested.

"Please—let me?"

And so she did. With her mouth, her hands and all the love that spilled from her swollen, aching heart, she brought him pleasure and peace and release....

Afterward they lay in a damp, exhausted embrace, a tangle of arms and legs and rumpled sheets.

Sophie knew he wasn't sleeping. Neither was she. She wondered about tomorrow and the nights to follow—would he share her bed then, too? Wondered if he would be here long enough so that they could truly make love, and then told herself that it was love they had made tonight. In the only way they could, and without the words, but he had to know. She'd never been very good at hiding her feelings, and she had never felt this way before.

Never felt as though one man and one man alone had been created for her, somewhere in time and space.

Only, why had he been created in Texas when her roots were here in North Carolina?

The sun was already blazing through the window when Sophie opened her eyes the next time. She sat up and swung her legs over the side of the bed, hearing Iris's fussing down the hall. Before she was even awake, her breasts had reacted to the sound.

Joe muttered something in his sleep and then the phone rang.

"Oh, darn these early-morning calls," she grumbled, wondering where her nightgown had gone, hoping he wouldn't see her stretch marks before she could find her housecoat. "Go back to sleep."

"I'll get it," he said, and he sat up, yawned and she saw that he had a few marks of his own. Scars, none of them new, but she hurt for him all the same. It occurred to her that the life of a policeman could be extremely hazardous.

She found her robe and was pulling it on even as she hurried down the hall. "Whoever it is," she said over her shoulder, "tell them I'll call back later. If I don't see to Iris right away, she'll get upset and swallow too much air."

Just as if last night had never happened, she thought wonderingly as she lifted the fussy infant from the crib. If she'd needed a reality check, this would serve.

She could hear Joe out in the hallway. "Joe, who is it?" she called softly through the door.

He kept on talking. Oh, Lord, what if it was one of those awful people who had phoned before? The same ones—she was pretty sure of it now—who had broken into her house?

But they were in jail, weren't they?

She thought she heard him hang up, but then he started talking again. "Joe?" she called just as he appeared in the nursery doorway.

She could tell right away that something was wrong. He had pulled on his jeans, but they weren't completely fastened. He was wearing neither boots nor shirt, and the look on his face told her that she wasn't going to like his news.

"I've got to go."

Sophie took a deep breath. "Well" was all she could think of to say. At least she managed to restrain herself from throwing her arms around his knees and begging him to stay here forever, to give up his family and all he'd left back in Texas and start life all over again here with her.

Carefully she slipped two fingers around her nipple and eased it from the baby's mouth, turning her so that she could nurse on the other side. She made no effort to hide herself. Under the circumstances, it would've been rather pointless.

Joe stood as if nailed in place, staring at her. "Sophie, did you hear me? I have to go back home."

"I heard you. What can I do to help? I'll be finished here in a few minutes, and then, as soon as I change her again, I'll come help you get packed. What if I make you some sandwiches for the—"

"You can drive me to the airport, if you will. If I can get there by eleven-twenty, I can catch a direct flight to Dallas–Fort Worth and be home by twelve forty-five, Texas time."

Joe could see the confusion in her eyes—those clear, gray eyes he'd come damn close to drowning in more times than he cared to remember. Still hadn't quite made it to shore, come to that.

But it would have to wait. "Miss Emma's in the hospital. She fell and broke her hip, and at her age it doesn't look too good. She's been depressed ever since she had that stroke last winter. Look, I'll tell you everything on the way to the airport. Right now I need to grab a shower and get packed."

The shower took four minutes. Packing took less than that. He cut himself twice shaving and cracked his bad knee on the bed frame trying to get his boots on without slowing down.

They made the trip to the airport in her old gas guzzler because she didn't want to tackle a stick shift for the return trip. Not with Iris on board. He could easily have left his truck in long-term parking, but he thought it might be a good idea to leave an extra set of wheels parked in a prominent place outside her house as an added security measure. He hadn't had time to get done all he'd intended. Not the fence. Not the cell phone. The guard dog was a joke.

He tried to answer her questions, but his mind was racing ahead in several directions. He was worried sick about Miss Emma. She'd been so damned close to giving up a time or two. This might just be the proverbial straw.

And then there was Sophie. God, yes, there was Sophie! Seeing her in the nursery, her breasts bare, the baby cradled in the crook of her arm, with the morning light spilling through the window, creating a golden halo around her head, he'd wanted her so damn much it was all he could do to stay focused.

He'd made coffee while she got dressed, and then he'd burned his tongue on the stuff. He'd walked out carrying Iris in her car seat while Sophie locked the door and hurried after him with his duffel. He'd forgotten the damned jade—the jade he'd driven more than a thousand miles to recover, and had to race back inside to get it, and she had laughed, but she'd looked more like crying.

Over him or the jade? he wondered. It occurred to him that if it weren't for a creep who'd made a career of fleecing lonely women and moving on, he'd have missed out on a vital experience. Might never have come east. Might never have met Sophie Bayard. Might never have known what it was like to be a father, even a surrogate father.

"About last night—" he said, and then broke off. What could he say?

"Don't give it another thought. We were both...we both—"

"Yeah." He cut over from 158 toward I-40 East and said, "Look, one of these days, some smart man is going to ask you to marry him, Sophie. If he's a decent sort and you respect him, think seriously about it, will you?" God, he could feel his gut twisting into a hard knot at the thought of another man's touching her the way he had last night. Touching her in ways he hadn't been able to.

But he couldn't bear to think of her growing old all alone. She was a warm, giving woman. She deserved a strong, dependable man at her side. So he made himself say it. "You need a man to look after you, and—"

"Thank you very much, but I can look after myself."

"—and Iris needs to grow up knowing marriage doesn't have to be a battlefield. That's important to a child. Stability. Just make sure he's the right one first, will you?"

This time she didn't argue. She simply nodded. He caught it from the corner of his eye and shot her a quick glance. She had that familiar look again—the rocky chin, the glittery eyes. He hadn't seen it for a while, but it was back.

They pulled up at the airport, and he remembered to give her the keys to his pickup. He told her to use it if her car broke down. Told her that he'd call tonight, and that once Miss Emma was on the mend, he'd fly east again to retrieve his truck.

"By then, Miss Fatcheeks will be sitting up, and you'll probably have a fancy job with all sorts of perks and benefits."

They both knew it was a lie. He'd be back before she was ready to go to work full-time because he needed his truck, but it was a way of putting distance between them. Emotional distance. The airline would do the rest.

He opened the door, climbed out and then turned back to say goodbye to Iris. She gazed up at him solemnly from the back seat. He curled a colorless wisp of hair around his finger, then leaned down, kissed her on the cheek and whispered something Sophie couldn't quite catch.

I won't cry, I won't, I simply won't! she vowed.

"No need for you to go inside," Joe said, retrieving his duffel and the shopping bag he'd stuffed the jade into. She looked so hurt, he had to take her in his arms. And then, right there by the parking meter, he gave in and kissed her the way he'd wanted to kiss her last night, but hadn't.

Hadn't, because last night had been sexual. This wasn't—at least not entirely. Hadn't, because if he had he might have made promises he was in no position to keep. His brain had been functioning to that extent, at least. After all these years his survival skills were honed to a fine edge.

With the taste of her still on his tongue, he walked away. From the queue at the ticket counter, he glanced over his shoulder a few times, half hoping she would come inside anyway, but she didn't. She'd taken him at his word.

Just as well, he told himself, and then said, "One-way, Dallas–Fort Worth, first-class if you have it, two carry-ons."

It was eleven twenty-five that night when Joe called. Sophie, who had given up and gone to bed at eleven, nearly broke her neck getting to the phone. She vowed then and there to have phones put into every room in the house, either that or get herself that cell phone Joe had tried to talk her into buying. He'd insisted she needed to upgrade her communications system, just as he'd pressed her to have a fancy burglar alarm, new locks on the doors and windows, a guard dog and a chain-link fence.

None of which would have prevented him from walking in, stealing her heart and then walking away again.

She shoved Lady aside with her foot and lifted the receiver. "Hello?" she said cautiously, hoping against hope.

"I forgot about the time difference. Did I wake you?"

And so they talked. Joe told her about Miss Emma's condition, and how long she'd be in the hospital, and what arrangements he was making so that once she came home she could get around.

He told her about Daisy's prospective new husband, a widower with two boys under ten, and what odds he gave the match, and laughed a little bitterly, Sophie thought.

And then he asked how Iris was, and she told him. How the dog was, and she admitted that Lady was sleeping on a blanket in the kitchen, but mostly, she was underfoot.

"Don't trip on her," Joe said, and they were both aware that they were talking all around the subject neither of them dared mention.

"Look, I'll call earlier tomorrow night, okay?" he said, and she told him he really didn't need to call.

There was a long silence, and when he spoke again, his voice sounded uncertain. Unlike the Joe who had struck her, right from the first, as confident to the point of arrogance, but in a nice way. A man who knew who he was and was comfortable with it, whatever the world thought of him.

"Do you want me to call, Sophie?"

"Yes! Oh, please...I mean, I really would like to know how your grandmother gets along."

"She asked about you. About the baby."

Sophie shifted the phone to the other hand, leaned back against the wall and smiled, feeling that same glowy feeling she felt when she gazed down at her daughter—the same feeling, or a variation of it, she felt whenever Joe smiled at her.

They said good-night soon after that, and Joe promised to call at a reasonable hour, and once more, Sophie told him he didn't need to feel obligated, knowing she would wither and die if he didn't.

One more time, she told herself as she slid her foot

out from under Lady's grizzled rump and led her back
to the kitchen.

Easing into bed again, she reminded herself he'd
have to come back for his truck, and she would see
him then. And until then, she would exercise every
day and have something done to her hair—a rinse and
a really good cut. And she would buy a few new
dresses, something for fall. And try that alpha-hydroxy
lotion to see if it would actually make fine lines and
brown spots disappear.

And Joe would find her irresistible and decide to
stay here in Davie County. He would get a job doing
whatever retired policemen did when they didn't actually have to work.

That was another thing that separated them. His
money. He'd never told her about it, but as the only
grandson of a woman who could afford to give away
more than a million dollars worth of stuff—no matter
how tacky and useless it was—to a museum, he'd obviously come from a background that differed vastly
from hers.

It was seven weeks to the day when Joe called from
the airport in Dallas and asked if she could possibly
meet him in Greensboro. His flight was due in at
3:47.

Sophie dropped the phone, stepped on Lady's foot
and yelled to the refrigerator repairman that the door
was open, to come on in.

And Joe, of course, heard it all and wanted to know
who she'd invited into her house. He groaned when

she told him, and then said, "Just be there, will you? And Sophie, drive carefully. I don't mind waiting if you're late."

But of course, she wasn't late. She was there long before the plane came in, her newly styled hair only slightly windblown, her new denim-blue silk shirtwaist only slightly wrinkled, the glow on her lightly tanned face only slightly radiant.

He dropped his bag and took her into his arms, baby and all, and she laughed and sobbed all at once. Iris protested.

"Sorry, Fatcheeks. Didn't mean to squash you."

It was after five when they got home, and then there were the groceries Joe had insisted on buying to put away, supper to eat and Iris to nurse, bathe and settle. It would be hours before they could even think of going to bed.

It was all they thought of. Joe examined the new locks, but his eyes never strayed too far away from where Sophie was. She put the sweet potatoes in to bake and set the butter beans on to cook, but she was aware with every sense she possessed that he was nearby. Lean, sun-bronzed, with just a touch of silver glinting in his crow black hair, he prowled and he watched until she got tired of dropping things and sent him outside to examine Lady's new pen.

Finally when the dishes were done, Iris was asleep, and Lady was outside, whining to come in again, there was nothing to keep them apart.

"I haven't been able to think of anything else in

weeks. Wanting you so bad—wondering if I've lost my mind—wondering if I imagined it all.''

Wordlessly she shook her head.

"Is that a negative? I don't want you? I haven't lost my mind? Or I didn't imagine it all?''

"Oh, Joe,'' she cried, and then they were in each other's arms, laughing, talking, tugging at buttons and zippers. The waiting was over. She would worry about tomorrow...well, tomorrow. For now, there was only this—only Joe.

Only Sophie, Joe thought. *Only Sophie could make me forget how bad things can be between a man and a woman. Make me want to start all over again, and this time to make it work.*

"Your knee,'' she said, and he drew back and stared at her.

"You're worried about my *knee?* What—you think it might be a genetic defect? That our kids'll be born with a bum knee?''

Burying her face in his throat, Sophie had to laugh. "No, silly—I don't care if they're double-jointed. I—'' And then she lifted her face to stare at him. They'd made it out of the kitchen and were halfway down the hall to her bedroom. "Joe—*our* kids?''

"I'm not even forty years old yet. That's not too old to start a family, is it?'' He felt younger than springtime. Whatever that old song said, he felt it.

"Joe, does that mean—are you sure?''

He took a deep breath and led her through the door, to the bed. Her pretty blue dress was unbuttoned, her hair was a mess—she'd shed her shoes, but she was still wearing panty hose, and those had to go. "Listen, I've had some wear and tear over the years, but all the vital parts are still working just fine."

"Prove it."

"So, if you're not afraid to… *Prove it?*"

She smiled that same slow, sweet smile that had rocked him on his heels the first time he'd ever laid eyes on her, when she'd been nine months pregnant and a prime suspect.

"Of course, if you're too tired," she purred.

There were challenges no man could walk away from and still call himself a man. Sophie was one. Had been right from the first, only he'd been too thick-headed to realize it. It had taken Miss Emma to diagnose what ailed him. She'd been the one to send him east to bring Sophie and Iris back to Texas.

"Too tired?" he growled. One step at a time, he backed her toward the bed. When the back of her legs struck the mattress, she toppled over, and Joe went down with her, letting her bear his full weight for a moment before he rolled over onto his side and carried her with him.

His shirt was unbuttoned. She made short work of that before she tackled his belt. By the time her nimble, capable fingers found his zipper, he was shaking like a leaf.

"Slow down, sweetheart. We've got all night."

"I don't want to slow down," she said. "Do you have any idea how long I've waited for you?"

There was no answer to that. He didn't even try. Instead they began to explore and to kiss, and then one thing led to another, and soon she was gasping as she took him inside her for the first time.

Take it easy, he reminded himself, gazing down at the lush perfection beneath him. Her breasts were ripe, their pale surface like satin, like warm snow. She was all woman—his woman. Joe struggled for the words to tell her how he felt, but then she lifted her hips and her hands moved down over his shoulders, lingering to toy with his small, flat nipples. They peaked instantly at her touch, and he groaned and thrust deeper.

He wasn't going to be able to wait—it had been too long. It had been forever. When her fingers trailed down between their bodies, and she touched the root of him, he sucked his breath in sharply between clenched teeth and carried them in a wild race over the finish line, where they collapsed together, laughing, sobbing—at least Sophie was sobbing. Joe wasn't sure what he was doing. Muttering something about love and terrific sex, and then more about love.

He suspected that from now on, he was going to be doing a lot of it. All of it. The words, the music, the whole ball of wax.

From the nursery down the hall came the call of the wild. Sophie laughed helplessly. "What timing."

"At least she waited, which is more than I can say." He was a little embarrassed at how quick off the mark he'd been, but then, it had been a long time. And she'd been with him all the way. He knew damned well he wasn't wrong about that. It had been her sweet response that had sent him over the edge.

"Stay there. Let me bring her to you," he said.

She protested, but not very much. Spreading her arms at her sides, Sophie stared up at her lover, smiling, and whispered, ''Oh, yes...''

Meaning nothing in particular. Meaning everything.

And then Joe was back, cradling Iris in his big, muscular arms, whispering, ''Your great-grannie's going to love you, dumplin'.''

And Sophie thought again, *Oh, yes...*

Epilogue

"A little more to the left," the tiny, blue-haired lady commanded. "There, that's better. Now, hang the rest of the stockings and fetch me that box of decorations Joe brought down from the attic. Daisy and that tribe of hers will be here any minute now, and if I don't do everything first, she'll try to take over. Bossy woman. Never could abide a bossy woman." She muttered something about an abomination before the Lord, and Sophie hid a smile as she hurried to do Miss Emma's bidding.

No one dared cross her. The old darling was as ruthless as any dictator, except where Iris was concerned. Iris, five months old, drooled all over her G'anny, and G'anny adored it.

Joe came in a side door just as she raced past on

her mission. "Slow down, it's still three days until Christmas."

"Daisy's on her way over. Miss Emma's afraid she'll want to take over the decorating."

Joe grinned and tugged his wife into his arms. "So let her. The two of them have been doing battle for years. Now that Daisy's got herself a husband and a couple of stepsons, she wants to prove her mettle. Miss Emma can handle it. Did you two get that newsletter finished?"

"It's ready for the printers. Now she's talking about desktop printing. Joe, I'm not sure I can keep up with her."

Joe laughed. His fingers were destroying her carefully styled hair—she tried so hard to look the part of wife of a successful businessman, but it was an uphill battle. He still delighted in reminding her of the way she'd looked the first time he'd ever seen her, sprawled out on her backside in her garden, as big as a walrus and going into labor.

"Oh, before I forget, Donna called," she told him.

His tongue was doing crazy things to her left ear. "Can she make it?"

"She's on standby—*ah, Joe!* She's...she's bringing someone special for us to meet," she gasped.

"Jeez," Joe said, and then grinned. "Hope springs eternal. I guess we Danas are late bloomers."

"Speaking of gardens—"

"Were we speaking of gardens?" With his hand inside her dress and his lips making goose bumps on the side of her throat, Sophie groped for her lost train of thought.

"By the way, we just closed on that piece of land north of town," he said. "One of these days you'll have all the garden space you need. We can plant row after row of jade and see what sprouts."

"What? Joe, how do you expect me to think when you're doing that?"

"What, this?" he asked, all innocence.

She gave up, mission forgotten, and surrendered to his kiss. It never failed to amaze her, the way her life had changed. And all because of a handsome, smooth-talking con man and a few chunks of carved green stone.

"Got a minute?" Joe asked. "I've got an appointment with a building contractor, but that's not for half an hour." He was doing wicked things he had no business doing in the main hall, where anyone could walk in and see them.

"No, I haven't. If I don't hurry, Miss Emma will start pounding on the floor with her cane."

"So let her pound. The exercise'll be good for her."

"Joe, you're totally heartless." She nuzzled that place in the curve of his shoulder that felt so good and smelled so good and always drove him wild. Driving this man wild was a newly developed talent—one she was very proud of. Maybe in a hundred years, the novelty would wear off.

"You got that right, sugar. Lucky for you, though, heart-stealing's not against the law in Texas."

* * * * *

**Help us celebrate
15 years of unforgettable
romance with**

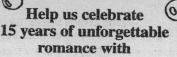

You could win a genuine lead crystal vase, or one of 4 sets of 4 crystal champagne flutes! Every prize is made of hand-blown, hand-cut crystal, with each process handled by master craftsmen. We're making these fantastic gifts available to be won by you, just for helping us celebrate 15 years of the best romance reading around!

DESIRE CRYSTAL SWEEPSTAKES
OFFICIAL ENTRY FORM

To enter, complete an Official Entry Form or 3" x 5" card by hand printing the words "Desire Crystal Sweepstakes," your name and address thereon and mailing it to: in the U.S., Desire Crystal Sweepstakes, P.O. Box 9076, Buffalo, NY 14269-9076; in Canada, Desire Crystal Sweepstakes, P.O. Box 637, Fort Erie, Ontario L2A 5X3. Limit: one entry per envelope, one prize to an individual, family or organization. Entries must be sent via first-class mail and be received no later than 12/31/97. No responsibility is assumed for lost, late, misdirected or nondelivered mail.

DESIRE CRYSTAL SWEEPSTAKES
OFFICIAL ENTRY FORM

Name: _____

Address: _____

City: _____

State/Prov.: _____ Zip/Postal Code: _____

KFO

15YRENTRY

Desire Crystal Sweepstakes
Official Rules—No Purchase Necessary

To enter, complete an Official Entry Form or 3" x 5" card by hand printing the words "Desire Crystal Sweepstakes," your name and address thereon and mailing it to: in the U.S., Desire Crystal Sweepstakes, P.O. Box 9076, Buffalo, NY 14269-9076; in Canada, Desire Crystal Sweepstakes, P.O. Box 637, Fort Erie, Ontario L2A 5X3. Limit: one entry per envelope, one prize to an individual, family or organization. Entries must be sent via first-class mail and be received no later than 12/31/97. No responsibility is assumed for lost, late, misdirected or nondelivered mail.

Winners will be selected in random drawings (to be conducted no later than 1/31/98) from among all eligible entries received by D. L. Blair, Inc., an independent judging organization whose decisions are final. The prizes and their approximate values are: Grand Prize—a Mikasa Crystal Vase ($140 U.S.); 4 Second Prizes—a set of 4 Mikasa Crystal Champagne Flutes ($50 U.S. each set).

Sweepstakes offer is open only to residents of the U.S. (except Puerto Rico) and Canada who are 18 years of age or older, except employees and immediate family members of Harlequin Enterprises, Ltd., their affiliates, subsidiaries and all other agencies, entities and persons connected with the use, marketing or conduct of this sweepstakes. All applicable laws and regulations apply. Offer void wherever prohibited by law. Taxes and/or duties on prizes are the sole responsibility of the winners. Any litigation within the province of Quebec respecting the conduct and awarding of a prize in this sweepstakes may be submitted to the Régie des alcools, des courses et des jeux. All prizes will be awarded; winners will be notified by mail. No substitution for prizes is permitted. Odds of winning are dependent upon the number of eligible entries received.

Any prize or prize notification returned as undeliverable may result in the awarding of that prize to an alternative winner. By acceptance of their prize, winners consent to use of their names, photographs or likenesses for purposes of advertising, trade and promotion on behalf of Harlequin Enterprises, Ltd., without further compensation unless prohibited by law. In order to win a prize, residents of Canada will be required to correctly answer a time-limited, arithmetical skill-testing question administered by mail.

For a list of winners (available after January 31, 1998), send a separate stamped, self-addressed envelope to: Desire Crystal Sweepstakes 5309 Winners, P.O. Box 4200, Blair, NE 68009-4200, U.S.A.

Sweepstakes sponsored by Harlequin Enterprises Ltd., P.O. Box 9042, Buffalo, NY 14269-9042.

15YRRULE

As seen on TV!
Free Gift Offer

With a Free Gift proof-of-purchase from any Silhouette® book,
you can receive a beautiful cubic zirconia pendant.

This gorgeous marquise-shaped stone is a genuine cubic
zirconia—accented by an 18" gold tone necklace.

(Approximate retail value $19.95)

Send for yours today…

compliments of ▼ *Silhouette*®
TM

To receive your free gift, a cubic zirconia pendant, send us one original proof-of-
purchase, photocopies not accepted, from the back of any Silhouette Romance™,
Silhouette Desire®, Silhouette Special Edition®, Silhouette Intimate Moments®
or Silhouette Yours Truly™ title available at your favorite retail outlet, together with
the Free Gift Certificate, plus a check or money order for $1.65 U.S./$2.15 CAN. (do
not send cash) to cover postage and handling, payable to Silhouette Free Gift Offer.
We will send you the specified gift. Allow 6 to 8 weeks for delivery. Offer good until
December 31, 1997, or while quantities last. Offer valid in the U.S. and Canada only.

Free Gift Certificate

Name: _____

Address: _____

City: _____ State/Province: _____ Zip/Postal Code: _____

Mail this certificate, one proof-of-purchase and a check or money order for postage
and handling to: SILHOUETTE FREE GIFT OFFER 1997. In the U.S.: 3010 Walden
Avenue, P.O. Box 9077, Buffalo NY 14269-9077. In Canada: P.O. Box 613, Fort Erie,
Ontario L2Z 5X3.

FREE GIFT OFFER   084-KFD
ONE PROOF-OF-PURCHASE
To collect your fabulous FREE GIFT, a cubic zirconia pendant, you must include this
original proof-of-purchase for each gift with the properly completed Free Gift Certificate.

Available in February 1998

ANN MAJOR

CHILDREN OF DESTINY
When Passion and Fate Intertwine...

SECRET CHILD

Although everyone told Jack West that his wife,
Chantal—the woman who'd betrayed him and sent
him to prison for a crime he didn't commit—had
died, Jack knew she'd merely transformed herself
into supermodel Mischief Jones. But when he
finally captured the woman he'd been hunting,
she denied everything. Who was she really—
an angel or a cunningly brilliant counterfeit?"

"Want it all? Read Ann Major."
—Nora Roberts, *New York Times*
bestselling author

Don't miss this compelling story
available at your favorite retail outlet.
Only from Silhouette books.

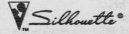